Albany County Public Library
Sources of Materials FY12

- County Sales Tax
- City Sales Tax
- Foundation
- Friends
- Cash Gifts from Public
- Replacement Fees
- Donated Items

PRAISE FOR **VARIANT**:

Publishers Weekly Best Book 2011
YALSA Quick Pick for Reluctant Readers

"A chilling, masterful debut. With its clever premise, quick pace, and easy-to-champion characters, Wells's story is a fast, gripping read with a cliffhanger ending that will leave readers wanting more."

—*Publishers Weekly* (starred review)

"An exciting, edge-of-your-seat read that combines psychological themes from works like *Lord of the Flies*, *The Hunger Games*, and *Ender's Game* in a truly unique way. *Variant* should join the ranks of today's must-read science fiction and fantasy series. A highly recommended addition to any collection for teens."

—*VOYA* (starred review)

"An intense journey with some of the most shocking twists and turns I've ever read."

—Pittacus Lore, #1 *New York Times* bestselling author of *I Am Number Four*

"*Variant* is a compelling story on so many levels. I loved it! The twist behind it all is my favorite since *Ender's Game*."

—James Dashner, *New York Times* bestselling author of the Maze Runner trilogy

"With *Variant*, Robison Wells explodes onto the YA scene with a brilliant nail-biter of a dystopian adventure. A breathtaking race for survival in a badly damaged world."

—Jonathan Maberry, *New York Times* bestselling author of *Dust & Decay* and *The King of Plagues*

"Benson's account unfolds in a speedy, unadorned first person. Hard to put down from the very first page, this fast-paced novel answers only some of the questions it poses, holding some of the most tantalizing open for the next installment in a series that is anything but ordinary."

—*Kirkus Reviews*

"Good old-fashioned paranoia taken to giddy extremes. Take Veronica Roth's *Divergent*, strip out the angst, add a Michael Grant–level storytelling pace, and you have this very satisfying series starter."

—ALA *Booklist*

"Filled with heart-racing action and suspense. An impressive debut with wide appeal, especially for fans of Alexander Gordon Smith's *Lockdown* and James Dashner's *The Maze Runner*."

—*SLJ*

FEEDBACK

ROBISON WELLS

HARPER TEEN
An Imprint of HarperCollinsPublishers

HarperTeen is an imprint of HarperCollins Publishers.

Feedback

Copyright © 2012 by Robison Wells

Library of Congress Cataloging-in-Publication Data
Wells, Robison E.
    Feedback / Robison Wells. — 1st ed.
        p.   cm.
    Sequel to: Variant.
    Summary: After escaping the walls of Maxfield Academy, Benson Fisher finds himself trapped in a town that is also under the school's control—where he discovers that Maxfield's plans are deadlier than anything he imagined.
    ISBN 978-0-06-202610-1 (hardback)
    ISBN 978-0-06-222830-7 (int. ed.)
    [1. Androids—Fiction.   2. Survival—Fiction.   3. Science fiction.]   I. Title.
PZ7.W468413Fe   2012   2012004296
[Fic]—dc23   CIP
                                                            AC

Typography by Alison Klapthor
12 13 14 15 16   CG/RRDH   10 9 8 7 6 5 4 3 2 1

First Edition

To Dan, Brandon, Ben, and Nate,
the guys who taught me how to write.

CHAPTER ONE

Jane stared back at me, motionless. She was older than I remembered—older than the Jane I knew. Her skin, which had always been smooth and perfect, was now freckled, and her cheeks and nose were red from the cold.

"I thought you died," she said again.

I shook my head, too startled to speak.

She stepped forward, and I flinched. I knew what she was. She may not have been Jane 117C, but she was something like that. An older version, another experiment. An enemy.

Becky was out in the forest, alone and dying, and I'd walked right into a trap.

"They're going to be looking for you," she said. "It won't take them long."

I paused, staring back at her. She was just like Mason, or Carrie, or Mouse, or any of the others from the school—she didn't know what she was. She thought she was helping me.

I took a step back.

"Don't go," she said. "We can hide you."

"No." I picked up the tarp that lay at my feet, the one I'd come into this barn to steal—something to keep Becky warm. I backed away from Jane, toward the door.

"Wait," she said, pleading.

"It's not true," I said, grasping the old wooden handle. "Everything you think you know. It's a lie."

I didn't know what else to say. How could you tell a person she wasn't real?

"Wait," Jane said again. "I know. I know about the robots." She unzipped her thin cotton coat and pulled it off. She held up her forearm.

From the pocket of her dress she pulled out a box cutter and held the blade in the flame of the lantern.

The ridge of her arm, where the bone met the skin, was speckled with dozens of thin scars—some smooth and healed and pink but others scabbed and new.

I couldn't speak.

"I'm human," Jane said. "We all are."

She pulled the blade from the fire and touched it to her skin.

CHAPTER TWO

Y ou can do this," I said, my arm around Becky's trembling body, trying to keep her on her feet. "Just over the next hill and we'll rest again."

"I don't understand," she repeated, her words starting to slur. As cold as it was outside, she was hot with fever. I could only guess that infection was setting into the vicious wound in her arm.

"We have to keep going," I said.

She nodded, but even that seemed half-conscious, like she was losing the strength to hold her head up.

"Fifty miles?" she breathed.

"We don't know that," I said. "That's just what we've always guessed. For all we know, we'll hit a highway in two or three miles."

Her eyes were closing while we walked. She was drifting away. She'd lost too much blood.

"Where did you get the tarp?" Becky asked. She'd already asked that, twice now, and I'd tried to explain.

"There's a town," I answered.

3

"Why don't we go there?"

"We can't."

"You talked to them? The people at the town?"

"Yes. We can't go there."

She was slowing, and I tried to help her walk faster.

"Do they know about the school?"

She slipped on a patch of loose leaves. I caught her, but she cried out when I grabbed her tight. The T-shirt that was wrapped around her wound was soaked dark with blood.

"I'm not going to make it," she mumbled.

"Yes, you are."

"Leave me here." Becky slid to her knees. Her eyes opened, wide and exhausted, and she tried to focus on my face. "Leave me with some supplies—the tarp, some food. Go get help."

"The school is looking for us," I said. "They'll find you."

"Then go fast."

"It could take days. I'm not leaving you."

"What about the town?"

I paused, not knowing how to answer.

Jane had cut her own flesh, the blackened tip of the sterilized razor blade splitting the skin and exposing the pink, bloody bone underneath. She'd winced, but hadn't hesitated. She'd done it before, dozens of times. Maybe hundreds.

Becky's eyes closed again, and I knelt next to her, taking

her dirty face in my hands to keep her awake.

"What about the town?" she asked again. "Did you tell the police?"

"They don't have police there."

I could feel her body shuddering against mine as she fought for air. "Why not?"

"We have to keep moving." I helped her to her feet, tried to force her to walk. Her weak legs stumbled forward, but she fought back.

"Tell me what's there." Becky was staring at me now, her face almost as white as the clumps of snow covering her hair. She didn't look scared. She didn't look worried or fierce or confident or anything. She simply stared. She was half-conscious. Half-alive.

"Jane is there," I said. "And others."

She blinked. "Jane is dead."

"This Jane isn't. She's real. Human. Everyone who was a robot at the school—they're a human here."

"It can't be Jane. It's more robots," Becky said. "It's a trap." The shock of what I was saying seemed to bring her back to her senses for a moment.

"She's human," I said. "She cut her arm. I saw the bone."

Becky looked at me, eyes wide.

"They're human," I repeated. "She didn't explain it all—there wasn't time. But they have something in their heads. They're connected to the robots."

"If they're connected to the robots, then we don't want to be there."

"No, that's not it." I didn't know what to say. I didn't have good enough answers. "She said they don't control the robots. They just—I don't know—they're just connected."

"It's a trap. We can't do it."

"I know. We'll keep going."

"They won't find me," she said, almost pleading. "It's snowing. I can wait here."

"If we don't keep going, you'll die."

Her body shook as she cried. We both knew it was true. She'd lost too much blood. I'd bandaged her arm, but the gash was deep and open—I doubted it could even be stitched closed, with all the exposed muscle and ripped skin.

I pulled away from her and looked into her eyes. Our faces were almost touching as she stared back, her tears clinging to her eyelashes. She was pale and gray.

"You're going to be okay."

She didn't say anything.

"I'm going to take care of you. I know that this sounds crazy, but—"

Becky's face turned to confusion, and she cocked her head. "Shh."

I listened, straining to hear whatever she heard. Her eyes weren't on me anymore—they were darting around the forest, wild and terrified.

"What?"

"Isaiah," she whispered. "He's coming." Her body tensed, and her hand gripped my arm. "We have to get back to the dorms. Before they lock the doors."

I felt like I'd been hit in the stomach. She was hallucinating. We didn't have much time.

I tried to speak, but my words came out shaky. "Becky, we have to run."

She nodded her head, her tears flowing again. "Don't let him get me. I'm not a traitor."

"I won't."

We stumbled forward through the forest. My tracks from earlier were completely obscured by the heavy snowfall, but I could smell the wood smoke, and in the growing light I could see the haze from chimneys in the distance.

"He'll kill me," Becky mumbled. "He was always worst to us. He said we knew better."

"Isaiah's not coming," I told her. "Isaiah's not in charge anymore."

She shook her head. "No."

"We left him back at the school, tied to a radiator."

Becky stopped. "You did what?"

Her eyes were different now; her whole face was different. It was like I was looking at a different person.

Jane had promised they could help Becky. I had to trust them. I had no other choice.

Becky's eyes were drooping, and I was carrying more of her weight now. "Can't you hear Isaiah?"

I peered into the forest. "We're almost there," I said. I still couldn't see the town, but it had to be close. She stumbled, and I tightened my grip around her waist.

I'd done this to her.

I'd done it to everyone. Isaiah had been right. He'd told me that I was playing a numbers game—that I didn't care how many died, as long as I was one of the lucky ones who got out. I'd told him he was wrong. That we would all make it out. That if we left as a group they couldn't stop us.

More than fifty had tried to escape, but only Becky and I made it. Some had died right there at the fence—I could still see the images of Oakland being shot in the chest, of Gabby lying on the ground in a pool of blood.

And they'd all gone to the fence because I talked them into it.

"Stop," Becky said, and pulled away from me. "Stop it. Stop." Her words were slurred, but for a moment her eyes focused on mine.

"We have to—"

She put her hand up. It looked like it took all the effort she could muster. "Listen."

I could hear my own breathing, steady and low, and hers, rapid and shallow. I almost thought I could hear my own heartbeat, but that had to be in my head.

Her eyes popped open and she pointed, but I heard it now, too. The engine of a four-wheeler, somewhere in the distance, behind us.

"Damn it." I dropped the tarp and picked Becky up in my arms. She buried her face in my chest as I hurried forward. I didn't bother trying to hide my tracks. The only thing that could help us was to get as far away from that four-wheeler as possible, to hope that our path was covered by the storm.

The moment Becky lost consciousness was obvious. Her body went limp, one of her arms falling off my shoulder and hanging loosely down.

There was a flash of red up ahead, the faded paint of an old chicken coop.

"We're almost there," I whispered.

Chapter Three

I stopped at the tree line, gasping for air. The town lay before us, silent and still in the rising light.

Jane stood in the doorway of the barn, just where I'd left her. It didn't look like she'd seen us yet.

The Jane at the school had been pretty, with soft, creamy skin and perfect makeup. This Jane—the real, human Jane—was harder and stronger. If it was possible, she was thinner now, the softness of her arms replaced with the muscle of years of daily manual labor.

She was still beautiful. More so, maybe.

Two more people appeared at the barn door. The first was a stocky guy with a rough goatee and a shaved head. He couldn't have been much older than me. He was arguing with Jane, gesturing fiercely.

The second, standing quietly beside them, was someone I couldn't forget. Unlike Jane, Mouse looked exactly like her robot version. Tall, tan, brown hair. Gorgeous and dangerous. She stood quietly with arms folded, ignoring the others and staring out at the forest. The last time I'd seen Mouse she was lying on the ground, her robot chest impaled by a machete.

They didn't seem to have any kind of uniform here. All three wore jeans and heavy work boots, but Jane had an apron on that fell to her knees and a thin cotton coat. Mouse was bundled in a leather jacket that was too big—her fingers didn't reach the end of the sleeves. The guy didn't even have a coat—just a thick long-sleeved shirt.

Mouse reached over and touched the guy's arm, and then pointed to me.

I took another gulp of air, and jogged out of the trees toward them.

As I approached, Jane put a finger to her lips.

"Let's get inside."

I nodded.

Jane's smile faded as she looked back at Becky. "Is she alive?"

"Yeah."

Jane walked in front of me, trying to inspect Becky's bandage while we moved.

"How bad is it?"

"I don't know. She landed on a broken log, and a branch tore her arm up pretty bad. Lost a lot of blood. And I think it's infected."

I expected the guy to help me with Becky, but he didn't even look at her.

"Are they following you?" he snapped.

"They're out there," I said, breathing heavily. "We could hear the four-wheelers. I don't think they've found our trail, or they'd be here already."

He swore and turned to Mouse. "Get the cows out and see if you can coax them into the woods to mess up the tracks."

Mouse nodded and jogged back to the barn.

I watched Jane's face as she fiddled with Becky, taking her pulse and feeling her head. She was acting like a paramedic, but I knew it was mostly an act. The robot Jane had been sixteen—this Jane looked maybe a year or two older. She wasn't a doctor.

"How long has she been unconscious?" Jane said, looking up at me. Everything about her was different except those eyes—bright, vibrant green. I looked away.

"Just a few minutes," I said. I felt a tear roll slowly down my cheek. With Becky in my arms, there was nothing I could do about it. I didn't even know what caused it—was it Becky? Jane? Was it that I'd accomplished nothing?

The guy pointed to my arm, his face cold and stern. "Roll up your sleeve."

I paused for a minute, confused.

"Put her down," he said, talking to me like I was an idiot.

I didn't respond. We were in six inches of snow, and Becky was unconscious. I wasn't going to lay her down.

"Do it," he said, taking a step toward me.

"Let's get inside."

His voice was steady and firm. "Those four-wheelers are coming."

Jane glanced up at me, and then at the guy. She didn't say anything.

Carefully I knelt down, wishing I hadn't left the tarp back in the woods. Jane's eyes met mine, and she sat in the cold, wet snow, cradling Becky's head.

When I stood back up, the guy was holding a box cutter. "Roll up your sleeve."

I nodded. I'd expected this—he was going to cut me just like Jane had done to herself. They needed to make sure that we were real, too, and not some infiltrators from the school.

I tugged at my sweatshirt, pulling it back to my elbow.

His face darkened and he swore.

"Are you stupid?"

"What?"

He grabbed my wrist and shared a look with Jane.

"What?" I asked again.

"The watch," Jane said, her voice hollow and small.

"You led them right here," he said angrily.

I stared at the beat-up watch, thinking back to when Becky had clamped it on my wrist the first day I'd arrived.

"I thought they just opened the doors."

"They track you," he snapped.

"We don't know that," Jane said quietly. She was talking to him, not me. "We've always assumed that, but we don't know it for sure."

"Of course it tracks you," he said.

"So cut it off," I said. I couldn't believe I'd been so stupid.

"It's too late."

I looked back at him, suddenly hopeful. "Maybe Jane's right. Maybe it doesn't track you. We were in the woods all night, but we're probably only a mile or two from the wall. If they knew where we were they would have found us in minutes."

He stared at me and then at Jane. It felt like forever. We didn't have time to argue. Mouse was herding the cows—five of them—past us. The four-wheelers could be here any minute.

I tapped my watch, pleading with him. "We'll cut them off, and then when they come looking for us you can say that we stopped here and kept going."

He lit a match on his pants and held it to the blade of the box cutter. "Tell me why we should put our necks on the line for you."

I stammered for a moment, not sure what to say. I'd just made dozens of others risk their lives, stupidly, and they'd all suffered for it. But if these people didn't help us, then Becky would die.

I took a breath.

"You're trapped here," I said. "Right?"

"Of course."

"What keeps you here? There's no fence, no walls. You all have a tracker like this? If you leave the town they'll chase you?"

The guy ran his hand over his shaved head and looked out into the woods. "Worse. So what?"

"So whatever it is, Becky and I don't have it," I said. "Cut off my watch, and I can help you escape."

"You can help us by leaving, now."

Mouse rejoined us, a heavy pair of gardening clippers in her hand.

"Here," she said, taking my wrist.

The guy held my hand steady. Mouse slid one end of the clippers under the metal watchband and then sliced through. It fell silently into the snow at my feet.

She then crouched beside Becky and cut through her necklace gently. Becky never stirred.

I picked up both the tracking devices.

"If you help Becky, I'll work on finding a way out."

He didn't move, just stood his ground. I could understand everything he was feeling—the paranoia, the anger—but I couldn't back down.

"She's human," Jane said, breaking the silence. She'd pulled back the bandage around Becky's upper arm enough to examine the gaping wound. I couldn't see it from where

I stood, but I knew Jane was inspecting Becky's bone and muscle.

The guy looked down for a moment, watching Jane, and then finally crouched beside her.

I wanted to say something, but it all sounded too argumentative in my head. I needed their help, so I needed to shut up.

Mouse bent beside him. "Where will we put them?" she said, her voice quiet and nervous.

He stared at Becky's wound for several seconds, deep in thought. Finally, he stood back up and grabbed my wrist.

"Don't move," he said, his face unchanged. He held the box cutter to my forearm, where the bone was closest to the skin. "This is going to hurt."

Mouse and the guy walked straight down the dirt road, which was visible through the snow only because of the deep ruts now frozen in the mud. Jane and I followed behind, Becky again in my arms. Maybe I was filled with adrenaline, but she felt lighter.

We passed farm buildings, chicken coops, rabbit hutches, and a few sheds before getting into the heart of the complex, where there were five green rectangular wooden buildings that reminded me of too many war movies—they looked like barracks for POWs.

Past them were two squat cement buildings, both of

which looked several decades older than the five green ones. The larger of the cement structures had a sign on its plain steel door that read, MAXFIELD COMMISSARY. The other, which had a row of narrow windows running along the top of each wall, read, WASHROOM. Steam was trickling out through a broken pane of glass.

"What's a commissary?" I whispered.

Jane paused, only for a moment, her eyes darting nervously from door to door. "It's an old word for *cafeteria*. Everything here is old."

As she moved in front of me, all I could think of was that night, only weeks ago, when the beaten and broken android of Jane had stumbled away from me and I'd learned the truth about her.

The truth. The concept seemed impossible now. What was the truth, and how would I ever know? I'd thought she and I had something. And then she was dead. But she wasn't dead—she'd never existed at all. I'd been friends with a computer program. I'd kissed a machine.

But now she *was* real. I didn't understand it at all.

The door of the washroom opened, and two girls appeared. They stopped instantly, and one reached for the door frame for support. I knew them both—Shelly and Tapti. Tapti—a Variant, like me—had revealed herself as a robot last night. Shelly was in the Society, and I thought I'd seen her fighting on our side last night.

The girls stared at us, gaping. I didn't know what to do.

"It's okay," the guy said to them, his voice hushed as we walked past. "Keep it quiet. We'll have a meeting later."

"Tapti was one of them," I whispered to Jane once we had moved past the washroom. "Like . . ." I stammered for a moment.

"Like me," she said, her eyes on the road.

I nodded, uncomfortable. "But I don't think Shelly was. She wasn't fighting against us last night."

"They went one at a time." Her voice sounded pained. "As they were needed."

"What does that mean?"

"The Shelly you knew was a robot. She just hadn't popped yet."

The guy shot back an angry look. We were being too loud.

Jane stood closer to me, her voice barely a whisper. "Most of the robots popped at the fence."

"What's 'popped'?"

"It's when the link between us and the robot is broken, and someone else takes control."

I nodded slowly. I'd seen it happen—the blank look on Mason's face when he attacked Becky, and when Carrie shot Oakland. They suddenly weren't themselves anymore.

In my arms, I could feel Becky's muscles tense and then relax again. It wasn't much, but I took it as a promising sign. She wasn't completely gone.

"Where are we going?" I asked. The road was dipping down into a dense row of trees.

"It's safer on the other side of the stream," she said. "Warmer, too."

I bent my neck, my head touching Becky's. "We're almost there," I whispered. "You're going to be okay."

She didn't respond.

The trees were hiding a small creek, maybe fifteen feet wide, and shallow. There was no bridge, just a ford, and the water wasn't entirely frozen over.

Jane ran across it easily, hopping from stone to stone like it was second nature. Carrying Becky, I didn't dare attempt balancing on the slippery rocks, and stepped through the icy water. It was only a few inches deep—just enough to seep into my shoes—but it sent shivers up my legs.

Jane paused at the edge of the trees and I caught up with her. Mouse and the guy were twenty yards ahead of us, continuing up the dirt road.

"There it is," she said. "Where it all started."

Breathing heavily, I stared at a large adobe building that stood in a clearing. It was only one story, but probably a hundred feet or more on each side—from where I was, it appeared to be a square. At each corner was a squat tower, two of which were crumpled and broken. The one door was enormous, made of wood and iron. Other than the door, the only break in the thick brown walls were tiny window slits every ten or twelve feet. They couldn't have been more than four or five inches wide. They had no glass, but a single iron bar ran up the center of each.

I'd seen this building a dozen times—or buildings like it—in every John Wayne Western.

"Fort Maxfield," Jane said. "You'll be safe here."

We crossed the field of snow to the door, where Mouse and the guy stood.

As we approached, I could tell this wasn't a replica of an Old West fort—this thing really was old. In many places the smooth stucco surface had flaked off, revealing the rough brown interior of the mud walls. Even the massive door seemed to be falling apart, and I could see some obviously recent repairs: one of the massive hinges was brass and shiny, out of place from the other blackened antique metalwork, and a two-by-four was nailed vertically up one side of the door to hold the decaying boards in place.

A wreath of flowers, long since dead, hung just above eye level.

This place wasn't anything like I'd hoped it would be. It wasn't safe; it wasn't welcoming.

The door almost immediately clanked and then swung open, revealing another guy—tall and skinny, his thick black hair dreadlocked.

"Everybody check out, Birdman?" the new guy asked.

The guy with the shaved head nodded. "They're good.

Take them to the Basement."

The dreadlocked guy looked at me and smiled enthusiastically. "I'm Harvard. Need a hand?"

I nodded, exhausted, and he scooped Becky out of my arms. I followed him along a rough wooden walkway.

The fort had a large open courtyard in the middle—now covered in a blanket of untouched snow. It looked like each of the four sides was lined with rooms, like a motel.

The farther we walked, the older the fort seemed. The adobe walls were crumbling and broken, and the wooden planks under our feet were cracked; about every fifth one was missing entirely. Harvard walked with careless expertise—stepping back and forth, left to right, avoiding weak boards without giving them a second thought. I copied his path, but even so I could feel the wood bowing under my weight.

As we continued around to the far side of the fort, I saw faces peering out of cracks in the centuries-old doors. I looked for others I knew, like Mouse and Jane, but couldn't really get a good look at anyone.

"Do they watch you guys?" I asked.

Harvard shook his head. "They used to try, but we keep a pretty good eye on it. We have people whose job it is to watch for cameras. We can't do much about the animals in the camp—you know about those?"

"Yeah," I said, even though we'd figured it out only the

day before. "Raccoons and deer and that kind of thing."

"Right," Harvard said. "The good news is we can keep them out of the fort. So far, we've never found a bird with a camera in it." He stopped and nodded toward a room. "Can you get that?"

I opened the door—the antique brass knob like ice—and held it for Harvard.

Becky looked asleep in his arms, her face calm, mouth slightly open. I could hear her raspy breaths as we entered a quiet, dark room.

"Hang on," a voice said, and I turned to see Jane catching up with us. She gave me an awkward smile and then hurried past.

Coming in from the white of the snow—even in the early morning—made it hard to adjust to the darkness, but after a moment Jane lit a lantern and the room filled with warm yellow light.

It was smaller than the dorms back at the school. The only furniture was a bed—narrow and low, like a cot—and a small wooden table and chair. A cardboard box at the foot of the bed was filled with folded clothes, and cans of food were stacked in the corner, under the narrow slit of a window. The walls were covered with drawings of all sizes, some on paper, others on large pieces of cloth. Some of the pictures were of the town—the fort, the barn, the stream—but others I knew well: the school, the cafeteria, the wall, and the gate. There were three pictures of Curtis, the leader of the Vs. He was still at the school, and I knew he was human.

Before I could ask about him, Birdman and Mouse joined us, stepping inside and closing the door.

"We're taking a big risk," Birdman said, looking at me out of the corner of his eye as he passed by. He shoved the bed to the other side of the room and climbed up onto it. "Not everyone in this town gets to live in the fort, but I want to keep an eye on you. Nothing you see or hear leaves this room, okay?"

I nodded. Even here there were secrets. That didn't surprise me.

Birdman lifted a large cloth picture—a mural—and I saw him prying something off the wall.

"There aren't many places to hide things," Harvard said, grinning as he watched Birdman. "But last year we figured one out. This adobe is thick. Most of the walls are more than a foot deep, but because there's a big fireplace on the other side of this one, it's more than four feet of solid adobe. It took us months, but we hollowed out the top part of the wall."

Birdman pulled a square panel loose and then slipped it into the hole it had been covering. He glanced down at me. "It's not perfect. If they look under the picture it won't be hard to find."

"Nice." I forced a laugh. "*The Shawshank Redemption*."

He nodded. "Except this hole doesn't get you anywhere." He motioned to me, still scowling, but some of the harshness was gone from his eyes. "You'd better get up there first so we can hand her to you."

The hole was high enough on the wall that even standing on the bed I could only just see inside. With one foot on the rickety bed frame, I clambered up into the Basement.

It was more like a cave than a room. The walls were all bare adobe—dry, uneven mud—and they'd laid down a few broken wood planks to serve as the floor. It was narrow, probably less than four feet wide, but almost the full length of the room below. The ceiling was low enough that I had to crouch to fit. At each end a tiny slit of light shone in.

"You call this the Basement?" I asked.

Jane handed me a stack of blankets, and Harvard spoke. "Just a little joke. In case someone overhears us talking about it. They'll think we've dug a tunnel or something."

I turned away from the opening and laid one of the blankets—the thickest I could find—on top of the rough boards.

None of this was supposed to be happening. This wasn't what our escape was going to be like. We should have been running, not hiding.

Harvard and Birdman were both on the bed now, with Mouse holding the cloth picture out of the way. They lifted Becky, and I gently pulled her in. I tried not to let her arm drag or pull too much on her shoulder, but it was an awkward move. My hand slipped off her wet sweater, and even though I caught her, the jolt caused her to gasp and groan.

But she was in the Basement now. I put my hand on her forehead, which was red and hot. Her hair was wet with snow and sweat, and I brushed it away from her face.

Jane climbed into the hole, a Ziploc bag of medical supplies in her hand.

Birdman looked in after us, speaking to Jane. "We're clearing out—need to make sure no one saw this."

Jane nodded, and Birdman stepped down. I heard the bed scrape across the floor as he pushed it back into position. Mouse let the picture drop over the entrance.

"There are vents that open up on each end, and one in the ceiling," Jane said. She was obscured by the dark, but I could tell where she was pointing.

I crawled to the end of the room and saw that the slit of light was a loose board. I pulled it out, creating a hole about a foot long and three inches tall. From here I could see the empty courtyard of the fort and the doors and walkway on the other side. Two girls were standing there, talking. I didn't recognize them.

Jane crawled to the other slit and removed that board. She spoke again before I did. Her voice was soft and pained. "I thought you died last night—both of you."

She moved back to Becky's unconscious body, but was looking at me.

"What do you mean?"

She forced a small, humorless laugh. "We can see some of the stuff our dupes—duplicates—do." She opened the bag, pulled out a pair of blue latex gloves, and began to untie the dark bandage around Becky's upper arm. "The last time anyone saw you, Mason was running behind and then his dupe popped. We thought he killed you."

"She fell on a log," I said, suddenly overwhelmed with exhaustion. "It was a broken branch—stabbed her."

"Tripped?" Jane asked hopefully.

I shook my head, the images replaying in my mind. "Mason hit her, and she fell." It hurt to even say his name. He'd been my friend, my roommate. "Is he here, too?"

She nodded. "But you have to understand. It's not the Mason you knew." Jane raised the bandage on Becky's arm to peer at the gash. "The one who . . . who did this—it isn't him. Isn't the real him. When he did this, it was after he popped."

She pointed toward a cardboard box in the corner. "There should be a lantern in there."

I dug through what looked like an emergency kit—matches, first-aid supplies, packets of crackers, a milk jug filled with water. Everything was covered in dust and grit.

The lantern looked antique—glass with a cloth wick—but it didn't seem too hard to figure out. I turned the handle to raise the wick like I'd seen her do minutes earlier, and then lit it with a match. A bright yellow flame flickered to life.

"No electricity?" I asked, moving the lantern over to Jane.

"Not here," she said absently, her eyes focused on Becky's bandage. "But there's running water and lights in the washroom and commissary."

"What's the point of that?"

Jane removed the last strip of cloth from Becky's arm and looked up at me. "Gives us more work to do. Keeps us out of trouble. Idle hands and all that."

In the full glow of the lantern, the gash looked bigger and deeper and far more violent than I'd remembered. It wasn't a clean stab—the broken branch had torn into Becky's muscle, ripping and tearing it. Her skin was caked with dried blood, but with the bandage removed the gash had begun to ooze again—dark red and thick.

My stomach churned.

"Is she going to be okay?"

Jane bit her lip and moved the light closer.

Somewhere a bell rang. It sounded like the old bells of the cathedral back home.

Jane's head popped up, and she looked into my eyes, terrified.

"I need you to do something," she said.

"What?"

"If I pass out, push me out of the hole and close it up again."

I almost laughed, but I knew she was serious. "What do you mean?"

"If you promise me you'll do it," she said, "I'll stay and clean her arm. If not, I need to go."

I nodded, though I didn't understand what was going on. Jane immediately turned back to Becky.

I wanted to watch, to make sure everything would be okay, but every time I looked at Becky's arm I was overcome—with nausea, with panic, with guilt. This wasn't right. This wasn't how things were supposed to happen.

Jane was working fast, scrubbing out the dried blood, the splinters of broken wood, the dirt. Becky was stirring, unconscious but in pain. I was at her feet; the Basement was too narrow for me to get up to her head while Jane was at Becky's side. The best I could do was lean across her, holding her good hand while Jane worked on the other arm.

Jane paused, looking at my fingers intertwined with Becky's, and then she focused again on the gash.

"You're going to need to rebandage this," she said, still scrubbing, using a toothbrush that she'd doused with rubbing alcohol. "It's bleeding a lot, but I think that's a good sign."

"What about gangrene?"

"I don't know."

"Is it infected?"

"I don't know," she said again, agitated. "I'm not a doctor."

She set down the toothbrush and picked up a small silver packet.

"What's that?"

Jane tore the top off and sprinkled a white powder onto the bare wound. "It comes with the supplies they send us. Good stuff. Amazing stuff."

She laid a small piece of what looked like aluminum foil over the wound, and then opened a packet of gauze. She looked up at me. "Can you help?"

I nodded and let go of Becky's hand.

"There are gloves in there," she said, gesturing to the bag.

The cloth over the entrance moved, and a face peeked in. Carrie.

I froze. The last I'd seen Carrie she'd turned on us, taking the gun from Curtis and shooting Oakland in the chest. I remembered the drawings on the wall of the room below us. Three of Curtis. This must be Carrie's room.

This Carrie was human. The one at school was a robot. That didn't help my nerves.

She didn't look at me. Her voice was timid and soft. "Birdman rang the bell."

"I heard," Jane said. "It's okay."

Carrie nodded grimly, and then let the cloth drop back into place.

I pulled on the latex gloves. "What's going on?"

Jane kept her eyes down. She pulled Becky's arm away

from her body. "Can you hold it like this?"

It didn't seem like enough—there were no stitches, there was no surgery—but as I held Becky's arm, Jane placed a thick gauze pad over the wound, and then gently began wrapping the soft white gauze around the arm.

Jane paused, and then looked at me, eyes wide.

"You—"

She collapsed, her body dropping forward. I wasn't ready for it, and I let go of Becky's arm to stop Jane from falling. Becky jerked in pain.

"Carrie," I called, then stopped myself, worried I was too loud. I laid Jane on her side—her eyes still wide-open—and peered out the hole into the room.

Carrie was on the floor, facedown by the door.

I swore under my breath, terror coursing through my veins. What was going on? Maybe they were all robots—turned off with the flip of a switch. I could barely stand to look at Jane; her lifeless, dead-eyed body was something I'd seen before, something I never thought I'd see again.

I remembered what she said, though. It didn't make sense, but I wasn't going to take any chances. I lifted her into a sitting position, and then pushed her feet through the hole. It was awkward and clumsy—I had to straddle Becky to get any leverage—but slowly I nudged Jane out, feetfirst. I tried to hold her under her arms, to lower her into the room, but she was limp, and my arms were shaking from fatigue, from carrying Becky, and from the cut on my forearm.

There was an engine outside—it sounded bigger than a car, too big to even be a pickup. It was getting closer.

I grasped her wrists and gently pushed her out with my foot. When she finally crossed the edge of the opening and fell, she jerked and I lost my grip on one of her hands. She dropped to the dirt, held by only one arm, and I knew immediately that I'd hurt her shoulder. But she made no sound, no movement. She was in a pile on the floor below.

The engine outside was louder, idling. It had to be in front of the fort.

I took the small wood panel that covered the opening and fitted it back into place. If someone moved that picture—if they wondered why Jane was where she was, and they looked on the wall above her—we'd be sitting ducks.

I blew out the lantern.

CHAPTER FOUR

Moving slowly on the wooden planks so I wouldn't make a sound, I crawled past Becky to the vent on the other side of the Basement—the one that looked out onto the road.

A short flatbed loaded with lumber had stopped in front of the fort's door. A man climbed out of the passenger side of the cab—and I knew him instantly. Iceman. The man who had directed us every day in the school, giving us our schedule and doling out punishments. I'd wondered whether he was a robot, like Ms. Vaughn, and he certainly looked it now. Despite the cold and snow he wasn't wearing a coat, just the same uniform he always wore on the school's screens.

He pulled a chain saw from the bed of the truck and yanked on the cord. It fired up on the second try, and then he walked up to the heavy fort door, out of my view. The saw whined briefly as it cut through something, and then the engine shut off. I heard the heavy thump of the wooden door slamming open.

Whoever was driving the truck—I couldn't get a clear look—put it into gear and rumbled forward, down through the trees and ford, toward the barracks.

Carefully and silently—almost too scared to breathe—I scooted back along the length of the room to the far side, to the loose board there.

I couldn't see Iceman in the courtyard. We were above the awning over the walkway, so while I could see all the doors on the far side of the fort, the rooms on the left and right walls, and the snow-covered courtyard, I couldn't see anything along this front wall.

Becky groaned, and I jumped. I slid back over to her.

"Shh . . ." I whispered, my hand on her cheek. She was burning up.

She groaned again, and her body shifted, accidentally putting weight on her bad arm.

Her gasp was muffled by my hand, clamped tightly over her mouth. My lips were almost touching her ear now. "It's okay, Becky. I'm here. You're okay."

She struggled, and I released my hand so she could breathe.

"You're okay," I whispered, almost pleading.

"Bense," she said.

"I'm here, Becky. I need you to be really quiet for a minute, okay?"

There was a crash outside. It sounded close.

"Where are we?"

My cheek was touching hers now, and I was still afraid that I was whispering too loudly. "We're okay. I'll explain later. Trust me."

"Are we safe?"

I wished I could hug her and tell her everything was fine. I touched her hair. It was wet with sweat, but still smelled a little of her shampoo.

"If we stay quiet," I said.

I listened for Iceman. I caught a footstep, or a knock, or a door opening. But there were no voices—from him or anyone else. Were they all like Carrie and Jane?

I could tell from Becky's breathing that she was asleep again. I sat up and touched her fevered face. I needed to go back to the wall and see what was happening, but I almost couldn't bring myself to move the six feet away from Becky. She was so vulnerable, so helpless.

I kissed her cheek.

Cold air blew in the crack when I returned to it.

Someone was lying on the ground. They were only a dark mass in three inches of snow—I had no idea who it was.

Iceman came into view. He stepped up to a door and checked the knob. It opened easily, and he disappeared inside. An instant later he reappeared, pulling a limp body by the arms. It was a girl, wearing a short-sleeved shirt and pajama pants, and he dropped her into the snowy courtyard.

She didn't move. Iceman reentered her room.

A moment later he left and moved on to get the kid in the next room. It was Mash, one of the Havoc guys. He'd never revealed himself as a robot back at the school. He was even at the fight at the fence, but had been on our side.

Mash was big—tall and overweight—but Iceman didn't have any trouble dragging him out to the courtyard and dumping him in the snow.

After inspecting Mash's room, Iceman moved to the next door. Two people were there—some guy I didn't recognize, and Taylor, one of the girls from the Society. I didn't know she was a robot either.

Iceman was looking for us, searching each room.

Had they seen our tracks? Had Becky's blood dripped onto the walkways?

He was going to find something—I knew it. And then what would I do? If I waited here they'd search until they found both of us. But maybe if I ran, they'd chase me and leave her. Did they know how sick she was?

Iceman reappeared and moved to another door. It stuck, and he shoved it open with his shoulder.

My heart was beating heavily. I felt hot, like I was going to throw up.

He pulled a girl outside by one arm. He didn't bring her as far as the others, and one foot leaned up on the walkway as her body lay on the ground. She had a coat on, but wasn't wearing shoes. Her long hair sprawled across the powdery snow and looked like spreading blood.

I held my breath as he walked back inside to search.

Becky made a noise—a deep, heavy breath—but I couldn't take my eyes off the dark, open door.

This was all my fault, too. Maybe the people who'd followed me to the fence had done so because they wanted to—maybe—but these people in the fort hadn't done anything. I'd shown up, and now they were being tortured and searched. We were all just trying to survive, but trouble followed me everywhere I went. No, more than trouble. Death and pain.

Iceman reemerged. He saw the girl's foot resting on the walkway and pushed it off with his shoe. He moved on to the next door.

From there he pulled a short, skinny girl and dropped her in a heap in the snow. It was Lily! I had no idea whether she was a human version of a robot Lily I knew, or whether the Lily I knew had been human and they'd caught her when she'd tried to escape. None of this made sense yet.

From other rooms I saw Mason and Tapti. There was a kid from Havoc who I didn't know, and a couple of girls from the Society.

I stared at Mason for a moment, trying not to hate him. It wasn't his fault. Or maybe it was. Maybe everything

Jane had told me was a lie.

Becky breathed heavily again, and I slid back to her. Some of the tension on her face had eased, but I didn't want her to wake up now. I sat next to her, poised to cover her mouth or hold her body still.

Another door opened. It was close. It had to be just on the other side of the wall, the next room over. I heard him drag whoever it was, something bumping sharply. And then he was back in the room. Something bumped, and then bumped harder. There was a clatter—maybe emptying a bucket? Or a box? And then a heavier thump and scrape, like dragging furniture.

And then quiet.

Carrie's door opened, and something below us crashed.

Becky's eyes shot open and she took a breath, about to speak.

I clapped my hand down over her mouth and looked into her wide, scared eyes. I put a finger to my lips and listened.

We heard one of the girls below dragged out of the room—the scuffling of Iceman's feet across the floor and the rattle of a body across the floorboards—and then he returned for the other. He came back a third time. Carrie had hardly any furniture down there, almost nothing for him to search.

There was a tremendous crash, like he'd thrown Carrie's

bed over. Becky's good hand clutched my arm. Neither of us was breathing.

He was pounding now—on the floor?

Voices. Dozens of them, outside by the road. I wanted to look, but didn't dare move.

The truck rumbled closer, following the voices.

Iceman's feet stomped around in the room for a few moments longer, and then he was gone.

I looked at Becky.

She mouthed the words, *Where are we?*

I leaned close to her ear. "I'll explain later. Stay here." I scooted back to the vent that overlooked the courtyard.

Everyone was awake again now, shivering and struggling to their feet. Jane had moved toward the center of the courtyard and sat on the crumbling edge of what looked like a well. She was massaging her shoulder. A few of the other girls sat next to her. Mason stood by himself.

I forced myself to look at someone else. Carrie was sitting now, quiet and alone. It seemed like the only people who were talking to each other were the people I didn't know. Everyone I recognized from Maxfield was stony faced and somber.

Others were pouring into the fort through the main gate. It looked like whoever was driving the truck had gathered the kids from the green barracks. Unlike those with rooms here, the others were all wearing coats.

I recognized many of them from school. Some I knew had been robots—Joel was there—but others I had no idea about. Walnut and Jelly stood next to each other. Had they been robots, or had they come here through detention?

"Quiet!"

It was Iceman, though I couldn't see him.

"Two students entered the town this morning," he said, his voice unnaturally loud. "They received help. Someone cut off these tracking chips. They were probably also looking for supplies, possibly first aid."

No one spoke or moved.

"The first person to give me information about these students will be rewarded."

Still nothing.

"Extra food supplies. New clothes. Heavier coats."

The faces in the crowd were looking down, or up, or anywhere but at Iceman. He seemed content to wait.

There was movement somewhere below, something I couldn't see and could barely hear. I glanced back at Becky. She was sitting up now. Even in the darkness of our hidden room, I could see the red splotches of fever on her cheeks.

"No one came," a voice said—it sounded like Birdman.

Iceman's reply was sharp and immediate. "The tracking chips were found in the barn."

"Then they went to the barn," Birdman said. "They probably found tools there, cut them off, and kept running."

Someone screamed, and almost everyone in the crowd flinched. A moment later I saw Iceman marching through the center of the crowd, dragging Mouse by the arm. She was fighting him, trying to pry his hand loose while scrambling to keep her footing in the wet snow, but he pulled her along as effortlessly as if she were a child.

He was moving toward Jane. I could feel my heart pounding in my chest, and my fingers curled into a fist.

Iceman threw Mouse down, and she smashed into the stone well where Jane sat. I could hear him plainly, even from the far side of the courtyard.

"Don't play games. We know you two were at the barn at the same time they were."

Mouse said something, and Iceman reached down and slapped her before she could finish.

Jane didn't respond. Everyone else was moving away, creating a wide circle around them. Mouse was facedown in the snow, breathing heavily.

I felt Becky touch my arm, but I didn't take my eyes off the courtyard.

Jane finally spoke. I couldn't hear. No one moved.

Everyone was looking at Iceman, waiting for a response.

I reached for Becky, and she took my hand in hers. Her skin felt burning hot—either her fever was raging, or my hand was bloodless and icy. Or both.

Iceman bent down and grabbed Jane by the coat, and

with inhuman strength threw her twenty feet into the snow.

Birdman finally rushed forward.

"Leave her alone!"

Iceman turned. Lily was at Jane's side now, bent over her, but keeping an eye on Iceman.

He spoke. "I don't need to remind you that you're at our mercy. You have two responsibilities here: to live and to not interfere with us. When you stop doing either, you will be of no further use to us."

Out in the courtyard, Jane was shaking. Her nose was bleeding, and she was holding her left wrist in her right hand.

Mouse was sitting up now, motionless, with her back against the well.

Becky's shoulder bumped mine, and I moved to let her look.

"Now," Iceman said, straightening his jacket and adjusting the cuffs of his sleeves. "Two final bits of business. We have left the first of several loads of lumber by the commissary. You'll need to build two more dormitories like the others. Hopefully, you'll do a better job with these than your predecessors did with yours. Remember—you're the ones who have to live in them. And the faster you build them, the sooner you won't be sharing rooms and beds with the new kids."

Birdman spoke. "More people are coming?"

Iceman ignored him. "The second item of business . . ." He scanned the faces in the crowd, looking for someone.

He found who he wanted, and pointed.

Dylan. I hadn't noticed him before—he didn't look at all like he had the night he'd beaten Jane. His face was gaunt and gray, and he stood expressionless and still, watching Iceman point.

Jane struggled to her feet, and then turned away, sobbing. Lily hugged her.

Dylan fell to the ground. There was no sound, no struggle. He just collapsed.

Blood spilled out of his ears.

Becky let out a small, "No," but her voice was drowned out by dozens of others. Some fell to the ground crying; others shrieked. Iceman ignored them all. He picked up Dylan's body and strode out of view.

A moment later, the truck's engine roared to life.

Chapter Five

Becky was sleeping calmly when I left the Basement. I didn't know whether the powder Jane had sprinkled in the wound was an antibiotic or a painkiller, but it definitely seemed to be helping.

"Where are you going?"

Birdman was standing a few doors down from Carrie's room talking with Harvard. Mouse sat on a wooden bench beside them, both of her eyes now black and swollen.

I stammered to answer, too focused on Mouse's face to think.

"Do you see why you shouldn't have come?" Birdman snapped.

"We'll leave as soon as Becky is healthy."

"No, you won't," Mouse said, her voice muted and pained. "You will get us the hell out of here."

Birdman touched her shoulder. He turned to Harvard. "When do you want to check out the perimeter?"

"It'll have to be tomorrow morning," he answered, "or late tonight. I don't want to go until this storm clears. And I want to take him by the Greens first."

"The Greens?" I asked.

Harvard smiled. "The kids in the other buildings. You were a Variant, right? Think of this fort like the Variants. Anyone who wants to live here can, but if you're here you fight. Greens don't want to."

Mouse seemed disgusted by Harvard's comparison of the fort to the V's, but she didn't say anything.

I nodded and turned away.

"Where you going?" Birdman asked again.

"I want to find Jane."

"Fifth door on the right," Harvard said. "And plan on tonight."

"Whatever."

I headed slowly toward Jane's room, trying to fight against the panic rising up in my throat.

"What's your problem?"

I turned to see Birdman following me, Mouse a few steps behind.

"I don't have a problem," I said, and kept walking.

He grabbed my shoulder and yanked me back, hard.

"You answer me when I ask you a question."

He was right in my face, maybe an inch or two taller than me. I could have taken him a month ago, maybe even yesterday, but I felt like I could hardly stand now.

The whites of Mouse's eyes were completely red, making

her bruised and blackened face look almost demonic.

I forced myself to ease my fingers out of a fist—they seemed to be clenching all by themselves.

I took a deep breath and then exhaled, long and slow. "What was the question again?"

Birdman's voice was ice-cold. "What's your problem?"

"You know what happened at that school last night?" I asked. "People died."

"Don't you think we realize that?" Mouse snapped. She pointed at her head. "We were there; a lot of us died. *I* died there, damn it. So don't pretend like you're some victim. You're the lucky one."

"I don't even know what that means," I said, throwing my hands up and turning away.

Birdman grabbed my shoulder again, and I spun and threw a punch. In one swift motion he deflected my fist and crashed his into the side of my head. I collapsed off the walkway and into the snow.

"Don't turn your back on me," Birdman growled.

"You're as bad as them," I said. "As bad as Iceman."

He grabbed Mouse by the arm and shoved her toward me. "Look at her face, kid. This is your fault, just for showing up." He towered in front of me, looking down menacingly. "I'm going to get everyone out of here, whether you help or not. But if you're not helping, then get the hell out of my town. We have enough problems without you and your sick girlfriend."

My head ached and my legs wobbled as I stood up. "You think you're doing everyone a favor," I said. "But you're just getting them killed. Their blood's going to be on your hands if you lead them to die. Just like . . . Just like . . ." I didn't finish. But I could see the faces of everyone I'd killed, as I talked them into an ambush. We couldn't fight this place, not when they could do the things Iceman did.

I noticed Harvard down the walkway, watching me.

I wished I'd never brought Becky here, wished I'd never taken her out of the school. Wished that I'd never even found out Jane was an android.

I headed for her room.

Jane's room was the same size as Carrie's, but looked much more lived-in. Her table was covered with knickknacks—figures carved out of wood or soap, pinwheels made from tin cans, clay sculptures. The walls were painted in bright colors, murals of skyscrapers and bridges and trees. In one corner were stacked boxes that looked like the entire town's stash of medical supplies.

I leaned back against the adobe. It felt cool, even through my sweatshirt.

Jane was absently massaging her wrist, looking down.

"Is this Baltimore?" I asked, gesturing to the walls.

The corners of her mouth lifted. "You remembered."

I couldn't bring myself to smile back. I had come here for a reason. "Yeah. Why did they kill Dylan?"

Her grin faded slowly. "It's this thing in our heads," she said. She looked back down and picked lint balls off her quilt. "It screws you up."

I watched her as she fiddled with the blanket, her fingers red from cold. She didn't want to talk about Dylan, but I needed to know.

"But why do they care if he's screwed up?" I asked. "You're all prisoners—I bet everybody's screwed up."

"Oh," she said, her voice shaking. "It's different. Are you hungry?"

I sat on the edge of the bed and reached for her hand, taking it in mine. She was cold, her fingers rough from years of exposure and work.

Her eyes met mine just before she fell apart, sobbing.

I scooted across the bed and sat beside her. I wrapped my good arm around her shoulders and she fell into me, shuddering as she cried.

She wasn't the Jane I knew, but right then I wanted to hold her forever. I bent my face into her hair, breathing her in and remembering.

"The Jane at school," I said. "How much of her was you?"

She gasped a halting breath that almost sounded like a

laugh. Her fingers curled into my sweatshirt.

"I don't know," she said. "I didn't see everything. I didn't control her."

"How does it work?"

She leaned back slightly, her head still on my shoulder, but more relaxed.

"The dupes have some kind of artificial intelligence that controls everything the dupe does."

"Then how are you connected?"

"Emotions," she said, and squeezed my hand. "Some memories and personality, but the main thing is emotions. And you have to remember—we're guessing on a lot of this. Maxfield never explained it."

"So the Jane I knew wasn't you."

"We started at the same point," Jane said, exhaling long and slow. "They put this thing in your head and make your dupe, and they transfer memories to the dupe. Not everything, but the big things."

"Like Baltimore," I said. "And were you really homeless?"

"Off and on," she said, and quickly moved on, not wanting to talk about it. "So, two and a half years ago, we were pretty much the same. The only thing that I had to do with the dupe was give her emotions."

"She felt what you felt? Feel?"

"Harvard's guess is that when the dupe needs to feel an emotional response—fear or anger or sadness—the implant in my head tells it what to do."

"So when the dupe saw something scary, it would ask your brain how to react, and you'd tell it to be scared?"

"Pretty much. But it's weirder than that. She felt what I felt, but I felt what she felt."

"What do you mean?"

Jane laughed, a fat tear rolling down her cheek. "I don't know what I mean. I can only tell you how it feels. When that Jane was really happy, I could feel her happiness. That's when I'd see things in the school. Whenever the emotion was really strong."

"How does that work?"

"I don't know. Sometimes it was like seeing through her eyes—like I'd go blind and see only what the dupe could see; that happened when the emotion was the strongest. Other times I was just kind of . . . aware of what was going on. I would know something was happening, but I couldn't really see it—like I'd be lying here in bed, but I'd hear conversations my dupe was having, or I'd know what she was doing. And sometimes I wouldn't see anything, but I'd dream about it later. And when all of us get together and talk about the dreams, there are similarities, so some things in our dreams are real, too."

"So what *did* you see?"

"A lot," she said. "It went in waves. There were some good times, and a lot of bad ones. During the war, I was aware of my dupe almost all the time."

I leaned my head against the wall. It was hard to imagine—that so many of the people I'd known there hadn't been real, but *someone* was inside of them, somehow.

"I remember you," she said, finally. "Those times with you were my favorite times there. I was aware of you a lot."

I didn't answer. Becky was on the other side of the fort, sick and hurting.

"There were times—" Jane said, and then stopped.

"What?"

"It's stupid." She was still leaning against me, but she straightened up a little.

"What is it?"

She looked down again, at our intertwined fingers.

"I just sometimes wished I was back at the school."

I wanted to say something, but I didn't know what. So I changed the subject.

"What's the last thing you remember?"

I could feel her stop breathing. She seemed to be frozen, long enough that I started to wonder whether Iceman had come back. But when I pulled back to look at her she just wiped her red eyes.

"I remember almost everything from that night, from that whole day. I remember when we found out Lily was gone, and getting ready for the dance." She laughed, embarrassed.

"I remember you asking me—my dupe—to the dance."

"And the end?"

She just nodded. "All of it. I was with you, and then Laura and Dyl—" Her voice broke on his name.

I squeezed her hand and waited.

"That's why they killed him," she said, her voice barely a whisper. She looked up at me, our faces inches apart as she spoke. "We were friends here, me and Dylan. He hated what his dupe was like, but he couldn't do anything about it. Dylan—the real Dylan—was angry sometimes; he had a temper. And his dupe turned that into something awful. His dupe was a murderer."

She paused, trying to collect herself.

"I wasn't the first," she whispered. "He'd killed others. During the war, working for Isaiah."

"I didn't know."

Jane shook her head. "No one at the school did, except Isaiah. But the real Dylan—the Dylan here—knew, and it was eating him up. It was a cycle—he hated what his dupe was doing, so he'd get angrier, and his dupe would feed off that anger and do worse and worse things. When his dupe killed me, Dylan couldn't handle it."

She let go of me to rub her face with both hands.

"We told him that it wasn't him, but he wouldn't believe it. He said that if his emotions had made the dupe commit murder, then it was his fault. He left the fort. Sometimes he'd sleep outside, sometimes in the barn. And he wouldn't talk to anyone. He stopped eating."

"They didn't have to kill him."

"Did you hear Iceman today?" she asked, her voice gaining some strength. "We only have two rules. We're supposed to stay out of trouble, and we're supposed to live our lives."

I nodded. "I thought that was weird."

"That's the most important thing here." She wasn't crying anymore. She was angry, filled with rage. "They killed Dylan because he was so depressed, almost catatonic. We warned him—we tried to help him, but he wouldn't take it."

"Why do they care?"

"Because they can't make a dupe out of you unless you're emotionally healthy—at least enough so that your dupe can act normal. The school couldn't do anything with Dylan anymore, so they killed him."

CHAPTER SIX

We stepped outside and Jane closed the door. The snow had stopped, but wind was rushing across the courtyard, throwing powdery specks of ice through the air like glitter. Jane said there was a meeting we had to go to.

"Benson!"

I turned to see Lily coming out of a door on the other side of the fort. She ran across the courtyard, kicking up snow as she went.

"Causing trouble wherever you go, huh?" she asked, grinning.

I paused. "Are you . . ."

"The real deal," she said. "I was human there; I'm human here."

"So you went over the wall?"

She nodded. "Made it a lot farther than you did before they caught me."

I smiled. "They haven't caught me yet."

Lily had been the best paintball player at the school, an expert at camouflage, fast and clever. If anyone could have gotten out of the forest, it was her.

"The school told us you died." I stepped forward to hug her.

"I know," she said with a smirk. "I hear it caused all sorts of problems." She looked at Jane, who smiled quietly.

"C'mon." Jane nudged me. "Let's get out of the cold."

The meeting room was near the front door of the fort. It looked to be about the size of four or five of the bedrooms put together, with heavy timber beams supporting the roof, and eight wooden benches facing a podium at the far end. It reminded me of a church.

We were the first to arrive, and Lily set about lighting the lanterns. Jane adjusted the small drapes that covered each window. They didn't look to be decorative as much as functional—heavy dark wool to cover each of the narrow slits.

"So what about the others?" I asked, watching them as they worked. "Mouse was back at the school, but what about Birdman? Where's his dupe?"

"He has one," Jane said. "It just isn't active. A lot of people are like that. The school has dupes of everyone here, but they only use them when they need them."

I sat down on one of the benches, exhausted. I still hadn't slept. "I bet you're glad to have it out of your head."

Jane exchanged a quick look with Lily.

Lily plopped down beside me.

"It's not like that," Lily said, her voice hushed even

though we both knew Jane was listening. "They say it sucks when your dupe dies. It's like *you* die."

Jane looked over with a slight smile. "Well, it's not exactly like that. But it sucks."

Lily put her foot up on the bench in front of us. "You have to understand—you feel everything they feel. When your dupe is afraid, you're afraid. When it's sad, you're sad. And you can't do anything about it."

"That sounds awful." I rubbed my hands over my tired face as Jane came over and sat in front of me.

"It's not always bad," she said quietly.

There was a pause. She wanted to say more, and I could guess what it was.

Lily jumped in. "Someone told me it's like a drug."

Jane laughed—finally, a real laugh. "It's not like a drug. But it's like . . . I don't know. You have this other life, where you have other friends, and whenever you're with them things are really intense. And then, suddenly, it's all gone. It's over. You'll never see—" She looked at me and stopped.

"I've only seen dreams so far," Lily said.

I looked over at her, and I was surprised to see a tear in her eye. She rubbed it away and made a face.

"There's a dupe of you?"

She nodded. "Yep. I told you, they don't keep you here unless they've made a dupe of you."

"So where is it? What's it doing?"

Before she could answer, the door opened. Cold air blew into the room and people began to walk in.

I recognized a lot of them. Mason looked at me long enough to open his mouth like he was going to say something, but then passed my bench and moved up to the front. Joel actually waved before moving on, and I wondered whether he knew that I'd been the one who'd killed him— well, killed his dupe after he'd turned on us. I'd stabbed him with a pair of garden shears.

I noticed that several who were coming in were holding gauze on their arms. Someone must have been at the door, checking everyone with a box cutter.

Laura entered the room, and I turned to Lily. "Is that the real Laura? The one who went to detention?"

"She's true blue, the same one you knew," Lily said. She lowered her voice even more. "We were in detention together—she showed up the day after I did. The little princess thought she'd get rewarded for what she did to . . . well, for what she did."

Laura wasn't like Dylan. She didn't look depressed or guilty. Instead, she held her head high as she made her way to the front of the room.

I knew she was goading me, but it was working. Dylan thought he was guilty because his dupe had done something, but Laura actually had—she'd been there. She'd tried to kill me.

Jane put her hand on mine, and I realized it had been clenched in a fist.

"It's okay," she said softly.

"I was there," I whispered, my chest tight.

"So was I." There was bitterness in Jane's words, but I couldn't tell whether it was because of me or Laura.

Lily leaned over. "Don't worry about Laura," she said. "Look."

I hadn't noticed while she'd walked, but as Laura turned to sit, I saw her wrists were wrapped tightly in chains. Mouse strung another chain from Laura's shackles to a round metal loop in the wall.

I didn't have time to ask who had punished her—Maxfield or this town—because Birdman was standing up now, glaring for the room to quiet down.

I glanced around, getting a full look at the crowd. I counted about forty, and I recognized maybe half from the school. I noticed Jelly and Walnut sitting together in the back, which now made, at most, four people who I actually knew from the school—four people who were humans there, not dupes.

"Pipe down," Birdman shouted, and the room quieted almost instantly. He looked at Harvard, who was standing by the door. "Who's missing?"

"Carrie. And we've got Lance, Chris, Kaitlyn, and Trena out on watch."

Birdman nodded and scanned the crowd. He laid a large piece of cloth over the podium and pulled a pencil from his shirt pocket.

"You all know Benson Fisher and Becky Allred are here. Let's get one thing clear: no one is going to say a word about them outside this room. They're valuable, and anyone who screws that up will regret it. Got that?"

No one said anything, though I saw a few heads nodding.

"Okay," he continued. "Let's hear today's reports, and we'll see if he can fill in a few gaps. Anyone pop since last night?"

One girl, sitting near the front, timidly raised her hand. I recognized her from the Society—Taylor. She was one of the younger ones. The only thing I remembered about her was that she was always smiling. That was how the Society was—they were either smiling and carefree or scowling with disapproval.

Birdman pointed to her, and wrote on his cloth. "What happened?"

Her voice was small. "It was late last night," Taylor started. "I saw it all—I was scared. Everyone was getting herded into the detention room."

Lily whispered, "After the fence last night, they rounded up the survivors and sent them back to school. We figured they were going down to detention."

"What's down there?"

Lily smirked. "It's where the magic happens. You go there and they stick an implant in your head and make your dupe."

Taylor spoke again, her voice quavering. "Not everyone could fit in the room at once, so they were taking them down in shifts."

"Who was?" Birdman asked.

"Ms. Vaughn was there," Taylor said. "And the other dupes who had popped. Tapti, Hog, Mash . . . and I think Grace? Anyway, everyone had gone to detention and I was in the final group. There were about ten of us. It was . . . It was scary."

Birdman was taking notes on all this, and there was no emotion in his voice when he talked. "Then what?"

"One of the dupes went down to detention with each group, so only Mash and Ms. Vaughn were left with us. Four of us—of them—tried to jump the dupes."

"Who?"

"Me and three V's," she said.

It felt like the air got sucked out of my lungs. Jane's grip on my hand tightened.

"Hector, Anna, and Catherine," Taylor said.

Birdman wrote the names on the cloth, and then looked up. "And?"

"Anna had a knife. I don't know where she got it. She stabbed Ms. Vaughn." Taylor paused. The room was completely silent. "That's all I remember. That's when I popped."

He nodded, jotting down more notes while the room waited. Shelly raised her hand, and when Birdman finally looked up he called on her.

"Hector is dead," she said.

Lily swore. I felt like I'd been punched in the gut. As far as I could tell, Hector—the Hector who I'd known—had been human. He died for real.

Even Birdman looked shocked. "You're sure?"

Shelly nodded. Taylor turned, the horrified look on her face obvious. She was wondering whether she'd done it. Birdman spoke before she could.

"You haven't popped?"

Shelly shook her head. "Not yet. My dupe is still down there."

"How'd Hector die?"

It took her a long time to answer, and after several seconds Taylor stood and left the meeting.

"It wasn't really Taylor, though," I said, whispering to Jane. "It wasn't even her emotions making the dupe do it, right? She'd popped, so it was just the artificial intelligence."

Jane nodded. "That doesn't help much, though."

"It should." I could feel the rage building inside me. The school wasn't just imprisoning people anymore, wasn't just killing them. It was tearing apart their minds.

Lily responded instead of Jane. "It's like what we said about losing your dupe. It sucks. Taylor just lost hers last

60

night, and now she knows it killed her friend."

"Hector wasn't her friend," I said angrily. "She was Society."

Jane's look was dark and cold. "You can drop that crap right now," she hissed. "The gangs don't mean a thing here."

She was wrong. No matter what Jane said, this town was divided. Birdman kept the people he could trust in the fort with him, and didn't believe anyone was human unless they proved it with a blade. Maybe there weren't gangs, but this wasn't a utopia.

Birdman tapped his pencil on the cloth again. "Who else is still active?"

Seven people, including Shelly, raised their hands. I knew who they all were, though none of them well. Only one was a V. Most were Havoc kids.

"Anyone want to report?"

Mucus, a fat Havoc kid, raised his hand. "We're all underground now. I was in the second group sent down to detention, and they took us to the cells."

"Individual or group?" Birdman asked without looking up.

"Group."

Harvard spoke from the back of the room. "I don't think there're enough individual cells to handle that many people."

I turned to Lily. "How do they know that?"

She smiled. "That's the whole point of these meetings. Everyone who's in this town has gone down the detention elevator and into the big underground complex beneath the school. When I got here they grilled me about it. They've made a whole map."

"What's the point?"

Lily shrugged. "Knowledge is power, I guess. Gather as much as you can. In case we ever get taken back there."

Birdman was still interrogating Mucus. "What's happening there now?"

He shook his head. "Don't know. My dupe is sleeping, I think."

"Anyone gone to surgery yet?"

"Not that I know of."

Birdman looked around the room. "Anyone else seen something different?"

Stephanie, the final active V, spoke. "They treated the wounded, but it was there in the cell block."

This was what I wanted to know—what I needed to know. "Who died last night—the humans, I mean?"

All eyes in the room turned on me. Birdman looked down at his cloth.

"What about Curtis?" I continued. "And Gabby?"

"Curtis is alive," someone said. "He's bad, though."

Birdman spoke loudly, quieting the room. "Sixteen died."

No, that couldn't be right. I stood up, but my legs were

shaking. "Not dupes," I said. "Not people who popped."

"I know," Birdman answered. "Sixteen humans died at the fence."

He read the names. Seven from the Society. Six from Havoc. Three V's. I knew those people. They'd listened to me. They'd all been there in the foyer when we decided to take a stand.

"They're thinking Curtis might lose his leg," Shelly said quietly. "No one's expecting Gabby to make it."

"No," I said.

Jane stood and tried to take my hand, but I shook her away.

"You're wrong." I pushed my way down the row.

"Benson." It was Birdman calling me, but I didn't care. Harvard put up his hands to stop me, but I shoved him into the wall and threw the door open.

Sixteen dead. Soon Gabby, too, and who knew how many others.

I ran across the snowy courtyard to the other side of the fort and threw open Carrie's door. She jumped up from the bed.

"She's sleeping," Carrie warned, but I ignored her. Curtis's face stared down at me from half the drawings in the room. Carrie's dupe had been with Curtis for how long? Years? And Carrie felt every emotion twice as strongly as the dupe?

Did Carrie know what her dupe had done after it popped?

I climbed on the bed, pulled the panel out of the wall, and scrambled inside, my exhausted muscles pumping with adrenaline and guilt.

I let the cloth picture fall into place behind me, blocking Carrie out.

Becky was quiet, eyes closed tightly in a painful sleep.

I took her hand, kissed her damp forehead.

"I'm sorry," I cried, hiding my face in my hands. "I'm so sorry."

CHAPTER SEVEN

It had been dark for hours when I heard Harvard enter Carrie's room.

He pulled out the panel and peeked in. "Ready?"

I'd been lying beside Becky, watching her breathe. I'd forgotten I had somewhere to go.

"I guess." My muscles screamed as I sat up. I had no idea how Becky could sleep on these boards, loss of blood or not.

I pulled my Pittsburgh Steelers sweatshirt back on, and retied my shoes. At some point I was going to need a change of clothes and a shower.

"What time is it?" I asked.

"Just after midnight," Harvard said.

He moved away from the opening and I crawled out. A very groggy Carrie stood in the corner in a worn pair of blue pajamas.

"You have a coat?" Harvard asked. He was bundled up in a thick, well-worn parka and wool hat, and he had on leather work gloves with the fingers cut out.

"Just this," I said, pulling the hood of my sweatshirt up.

"We're gonna be out there for a while. Let's go check Dylan's room. No one's cleaned it yet." The idea of wearing Dylan's clothes didn't appeal to me at all, but as I stepped into the cold night air I realized it was probably smart.

Lily was waiting for us.

"Ready to stick it to the man?" she asked. Her breath came out in white puffs.

"Sure," I said, and followed Harvard.

"A couple things on the schedule for tonight," Harvard said, seeming remarkably cheerful. "First a coat. Then we're going to the Greens to talk to Shelly; then we're going out to the perimeter."

"Glad I can help," I grumbled.

"Man, I've been waiting for you for years."

"Why?"

Harvard stopped at a door. It hung open a few inches.

"Kid, you don't have one of these things in your head." He struck a match and lit Dylan's lantern. "You're gold."

"I thought Dylan moved out of the fort."

"He wandered," Lily said. "We always hoped he'd come back." Dylan's room was blank and empty. The bed was made, but rumpled, and Dylan's few belongings were in a cardboard box by the window. Unlike every other room I'd seen, there was nothing painted on the walls. In fact, they looked recently whitewashed.

"They always said detention meant death back at the school."

Harvard smiled. "It can mean death if you're stubborn and fight them. It probably would have meant death for you. But nope, they just take you down the elevator, give you an implant, and ship you here."

"We're a freak farm," Lily said.

I found a windbreaker. It was thin, but new and sturdy, and it was big enough to pull over my sweatshirt.

"I didn't recognize half the people at the meeting today," I said. "Why aren't all their dupes active?"

"Science," Harvard said, relishing the word like it was just as exciting to him as *escape*. "You don't want to load a school full of robots if you're testing the robots. Our assumption is that the whole point of the robots is to meld into the real world—to interact naturally with humans. If the school was mostly robots, then it would be a lousy experiment."

He pulled a pair of thick wool socks from Dylan's box and stuffed them into the pocket of his coat. Lily blew out the lantern.

"Where's your dupe, then?"

"The last time I was aware of him, he was in a dark room somewhere in the underground complex. It looked like a closet."

I looked over at Lily. She nodded. "Me, too."

We left the room and headed for the massive front door.

Harvard knocked on a door and got a kid I didn't know to follow us out and lock the gate after we'd left. Lily pulled my sweatshirt hood up to cover my face. They were still searching for me, after all.

"They're just waiting to use your dupes? Saving them for later?" I asked as we trudged out onto the snowy road. The mud was frozen solid now, and it seemed petrified, like the tire ruts were dinosaur tracks preserved in stone.

"I guess," he said. "There are a lot of us like that. And the implants do more than just connect us to the dupes. They trap us here in town, and they can disable us, too, like they did today—"

"Or kill us, like with Dylan," Lily said.

"So we all have implants," Harvard said simply. "I'm only aware of mine once or twice a month. I'm hoping they'll use it when they repopulate the school."

"Repopulate?"

Lily didn't seem nearly as excited as Harvard. "It's empty now. Everyone's underground getting chips in their heads. If the experiment continues, they'll need a new batch of dupes—and humans."

I didn't want to think about that. More innocent kids at the school. More screwed-up kids in the town.

I couldn't see the other buildings of the town yet—they were on the other side of the creek and through the thick stand of cottonwoods—but the smoke from their fires was hanging in the sky. I'd watched that smoke from the school. It was what had led us here.

"So what's the deal with Fort Apache?" I asked, glancing back at the moonlit adobe box we'd just left. "Jane said something about that being where it all started."

"It's a guess," Lily said with a shrug.

"A guess that makes a lot of sense," Harvard added enthusiastically. "Picture the whole complex. The oldest is the fort, probably built in the mid–eighteen hundreds. Then we have the washroom and commissary—maybe built in the thirties?"

"A guess," Lily added.

"It's all guesses," Harvard said, ignoring her. "Then the Greens' barracks, which are maybe forties or fifties?"

The shallow creek was partially frozen over, though I could see the smashed ice where the truck had driven through it. The layer of snow over the ice gave us plenty of traction—I didn't slip once as we crossed.

"We're not sure how old the school is," Harvard said. "But I have a theory about the history of this place—"

Lily cut him off, plainly tired of Harvard's long explanations. "The experiment started in the fort way back two hundred years ago. Then it moved to the school, and the humans stayed here to control the dupes."

"So when the experiment was here—when the dupes were here—where were their humans?"

Harvard paused, looking down the road.

"We have extra guards on duty tonight," he whispered, his mind suddenly elsewhere. "They're going to be looking for you."

Lily leaned closer to me. "We don't think they had humans before."

Harvard put his finger to his mouth, watching something, and then motioned for us to follow him down the dirt road toward the barracks.

"We think Iceman and Ms. Vaughn are older models of androids," he finally said. "Straight AI, no humans attached. But the AI wasn't good enough, so they couldn't fit into society—they couldn't blend in."

We stopped again, pausing in the shadow of the commissary while Harvard watched.

"I think we're good," he said, and started moving forward. "Keep quiet, though."

I didn't know what he was looking for, but I was glad Dylan's windbreaker was dark blue to cover up the white-and-yellow logo on my sweatshirt.

One day I wasn't going to have to watch over my shoulder, afraid for my life. Paranoia had become normal life, and I was sick of it.

We left the road. The untouched snow gave me confidence that we weren't walking into an ambush as Harvard directed us around the back of the buildings. Steam was pouring out of the washroom's broken windows, and I could hear the running water of showers.

I followed Harvard to the last of the barracks. The green paint was flaking off, exposing the bare old wood underneath, but it seemed sturdy enough.

He motioned for us to wait along the side of the barrack, and went around the front.

"Why do we trust this guy?" I whispered to Lily.

She smiled. "I don't trust anybody. I like Harvard, though. He's in charge of escape."

"I thought that Birdman was in charge."

"Birdman's in charge overall," she said. "Mouse is in charge of something, too, though I haven't figured out what. I get the feeling that she just latches onto whoever is in charge. That's what her dupe did."

Harvard's head appeared around the edge of the building and he waved to us. "We're clear," he said, louder than I'd expected. Whatever he was worried about, it wasn't here.

The inside of the building wasn't what I was expecting, either. I'd pictured tidy rows of cots, like an army barrack, but it was much nicer. There were rows of soft beds heaped with blankets and pillows, each with a dresser and lantern. Three overstuffed couches surrounded a community fireplace. The fact that anyone chose to live in the fort instead of the barracks was a testament to how paranoid Birdman was about security. Maybe Maxfield made the barracks more pleasant to entice people out of the relative safety of the fort.

Only a few lanterns flickered, and the fire on the hearth had burned down to coals. Harvard guided me to the couch, where Shelly sat wearing a pink hoodie and flannel pajama pants. Lily stayed by the front window, watching the road.

"First things first," Shelly said. "I won't say a word until you unchain her."

Harvard glanced at me. "You're going to make a big deal about this in front of Benson?"

She ignored me. "That has nothing to do with it. If you want my help, you unchain her."

Harvard glanced to the far end of the room, and I stood to see what he was looking at.

It was Laura, her hands wrapped tightly in heavy chains that were padlocked to the wall. She was staring back at me, quiet. Her eyes looked black in the darkness.

Harvard sighed, but lightly. Nothing seemed to really concern him. "She's a murderer."

"I don't want to get into it again," Shelly said. "Let her get off the floor or this is over."

Beds creaked as other kids rolled over to watch what was going on.

"Birdman won't like this," Harvard said, his smile eerily glued to his face.

Shelly cocked her head. "Do you think that carries any weight with me?"

"She stood trial."

Shelly laughed coldly.

"Fine," he said. "But only her hands, not her feet."

I watched him walk the length of the room, all eyes on him as he bent over Laura and loosened the chains from her hands.

She deserved to be in those chains. I'd been there. I'd seen what she'd done.

Obviously in pain, Laura stood, her fettered feet clanking against the wooden floor as she took the few steps toward her bed. Harvard kicked her in the butt and she stumbled to the mattress.

As she lay down, she flipped Harvard off, and then looked at me. "Looks like you chose your friends as well here as you did back at the school."

My muscles tensed. She was small, frail, and chained, and I wanted to punch her in the teeth. She deserved everything she got.

Harvard plopped onto the couch, grabbing the poker and jabbing at the fire.

Shelly finally looked at me. She was tense, uncertain.

"How's Becky?"

"Alive," I answered, sitting down.

"Shelly has some interesting news," Harvard said, sitting on the edge of the couch and slapping her knee. "Since you're the most recent to come from the school, we wanted to run it past you."

"It's probably nothing," she said, obviously annoyed with Harvard, "but something seems weird."

"Everything seems weird," I said, and she heaved a sigh.

"We"—she gestured around the room, but I assumed she meant the whole camp—"try to keep track of exactly what's going on at the school. Like the meeting today—Birdman gets us together every day and we write down what's been happening with our dupes."

I nodded. "So, what's the weird stuff?"

"Two kids," she said. "They're in the cells in the underground complex. It seems like they were there before my dupe got there."

"Isn't the underground complex full of kids?" I asked. "Everyone from the school?"

"I've never seen these two before," Shelly said. "I've asked around. No one who still has an active dupe has seen them before. We were wondering if you knew anything about them."

"How would I know?"

She scowled. "We only see snippets. You were there—you saw everything."

"Unless you can draw a picture of them, I have no idea how I'm supposed to know who they are."

Harvard poked the fire again. "No new students came after you, right?"

"Right."

Shelly ran her fingers through her hair and sighed, tired. "They're sisters."

That didn't sound right. "I never knew any sisters. No one at Maxfield had any family."

"These girls don't talk much—they're in the cell across from my dupe—but they're obviously related. They look almost the same, both blond, same face, same mannerisms; one is just older than the other. They're terrified, and the younger one clings to the older."

"How old?"

"Maybe thirteen and sixteen? I don't know. My dupe has tried to talk to them, I think. But they almost seem to have a pact of silence."

I shrugged. "I have no idea. Maybe they were scheduled to come to the school before we all tried to escape."

"We'll know them soon enough," Harvard said with a smirk. "They'll end up in the town once Maxfield gives them implants and makes dupes. But that's not the point. We can't figure out why they're bringing in new people and taking them straight underground. It seems like they have plenty of us humans already. Why would they need more dupes? And why sisters?"

That *did* seem weird. "So we're assuming that everyone in the school—everyone who tried to escape with me—is getting an implant and coming here?"

"That's probably why they're having us build more barracks," Shelly said, and stood. "Speaking of, I need to go to bed. We'll have to get to work tomorrow morning."

She looked down at Harvard, something in her eyes. Annoyance? Disgust? "I hope Birdman will be sending us some help this time."

"I haven't heard," he said with a carefree shrug.

From the back of the room a voice called out sarcastically, "Well, you can count on Benson to help. He's always thinking about everyone else."

I jumped to my feet and took a step toward the bed. "Excuse me?"

Shelly grabbed my arm. "Don't."

"You're actually claiming that I don't care about people? I tried to get everyone out."

Laura sneered. "Nice job, too."

"At least I tried. I'm not a killer."

"I was trying to prevent deaths," she snapped.

I laughed, because I wanted to break her jaw and I had to force myself not to. "You were trying to prevent deaths by beating Jane to death with a pipe?"

She paused, but her face only got colder, more vicious.

"How many died at the fence? Sixteen? And I'm the bad guy?"

I jumped at her, but Lily was in front of me in an instant.

"Slow down, big boy," she said. "You're gonna hit a girl?"

"She killed—"

Laura was on her feet. "That Jane was a robot."

"You didn't know that!" I shoved Lily out of the way, but Harvard caught me from behind.

"Let it go," he said. "She'll get hers."

Shelly had moved to Laura's bed, standing between us.

"This isn't over," I said.

"No, it isn't," Laura snapped. "You're not the only person who lost friends yesterday."

I threw Harvard off my back, but didn't move toward her. "Everything you did," I said, stabbing my finger at Laura, "every kid you hauled to detention, everybody you stopped from escaping, every rule you enforced—that didn't matter to the school at all, did it? When they hauled you underground—when they drilled into your head and crammed a bomb into it—they didn't give a damn who you were. Did they?"

Laura didn't move, didn't answer.

"*Did they?*" I screamed.

She looked shaken. "No."

"I hope it was worth it." I turned and stormed out.

CHAPTER EIGHT

Lily and I stood outside the barracks, in the shadows, while Harvard scouted ahead.

"Laura was on trial?" I asked, taking deep breaths to calm down.

"If you want to call it that. Everyone here knew what she'd done before she even arrived. She got to say something in her defense, and then they locked her up."

"She deserves it."

Harvard was close to the tree line, talking to another kid. He'd said there were always guards out there, day and night.

"Why don't you just run?" Lily asked, her voice low but intense. "You don't have the implant. They're already searching for you, and if they don't find you out there, it won't be long before they tear this town apart looking for you."

"I have to wait for Becky."

"We can take care of her. You go for help."

"No."

"Becky's one of the worst," Lily said. "Don't you remember? She was in the same gang as Laura. They were roommates. Besides, I thought you and Jane—"

"Things changed after you left."

Lily crossed her arms. "Apparently."

A few minutes later Harvard trudged back through the snow, smiling like it was Christmas morning.

"We think there are beacons," he said, motioning for us to follow him into the field. "Some kind of transmitters arranged all around the town, kinda like an electronic fence. That's why, when we get too far out, the implants hurt."

I shrugged. "I didn't see anything out there."

"It was dark this morning," Lily said.

"It's dark now," I snapped.

"You weren't looking before," Harvard said.

"Those kids in the school—the sisters," I said, changing the subject. "Why do you care? Just another couple of prisoners."

We had reached the trees, and Harvard stopped and fished in his pockets, eventually producing a spool of twine. He handed one end to Lily, and then measured ten paces to her right.

"Because it's weird, you know? It's not the way the school does things. Everyone starts as a human student at the school, and then they either try to escape or get sent to detention and wind up here. But those two went straight underground."

He pulled the twine tight between him and Lily.

"What am I supposed to do?" she asked.

Harvard's voice was excited, and he stared at the forest like he was a few steps from freedom. "My thinking is this: there's a series of transmitters somewhere out there, and they radiate their signal in a circle—well, a sphere, if we're being accurate. So you and I will walk toward a transmitter, and we'll each stop when we feel the pain. Presumably that means we'll both be the same distance from the transmitter."

Even in the dim moonlight I could tell Lily was rolling her eyes. "So?"

"So if we're each the same distance from the transmitter, then Benson will go to the center of this string, and then walk at a perpendicular direction straight into the forest. He should walk right into the transmitter."

Neither Lily nor I said anything. It didn't make any sense to me, though I admit my mind was elsewhere.

"It's geometry, folks," Harvard said. "Some of us paid attention in school."

Lily just looked at me and shrugged as Harvard began slowly walking toward the woods. She did the same, trying to stay in a straight line and keep the twine tight despite the underbrush and muddy snow she had to navigate around.

"What if the transmitter isn't out here?" I said, watching them. "What if it's in the center of town, and your implants hurt when you get too far away from it?"

Harvard paused. "Thought about that. But I can't find

anything in town." He began again.

After a moment—he was standing only a foot from the first tree—he stopped. "I can feel it."

Lily kept walking, taking a few steps into the trees and climbing over a rotted log before stopping as well. "Me too."

"Hold it tight," Harvard said, and motioned for me. "Stand in the middle and look perpendicular to the string— that's ninety degrees."

"I know what *perpendicular* means," I said, peering into the dark forest. Even the slightest amount of camouflage could hide a transmitter in this darkness. And I wouldn't know what one looked like in full daylight—an antenna, maybe? "I'll be back."

I entered the woods, my aching body fighting against me as I clambered over the thick growth here. I wanted to help them—of course I did—but this seemed like such a waste of time. We didn't even know whether anything was out there to find. Maybe the best plan was just for Becky and me to get supplies and run.

I was only ten feet into the trees when I heard Harvard swear. I turned back to see him looking somewhere over to my left. Lily was crouched down and alert, like we were playing paintball again. I dropped to my knees, shrouding myself in the brush.

For a moment there was only silence, and then I heard boots in the snow. I was so stupid. Of course they'd come looking for us again, and here I was tromping through an open field. How could I have left Becky back at the fort with only Carrie to guard her?

Something moved in the brush.

I tried to peek out between the tangle of sticks and briars, but it suddenly felt much darker than before—darker and colder. I was a sitting duck out here. I wanted to get back to the Basement. I *needed* to get back there.

"Deer," Lily whispered, much closer than I thought she'd been.

I exhaled.

"They watch us," she continued.

"I know," I said.

Lily scanned the trees, her eyes smart and vigilant. She was good at this—the best paintball player at the school. Most of the tactics the V's used had been hers, and her tiny frame hid her surprising athleticism.

But they'd still caught her. She was still a prisoner here.

Lily ducked back down. "I don't think it saw us."

"I should have waited a couple days before I came out of the fort."

"We're okay," she said. Whatever she'd seen—or not seen—had eased her tension. She wasn't on lookout anymore.

"We don't know that until the deer is gone."

The forest was cold and claustrophobic; every twisted

pine and tangled bush seemed to surround me like bars and chains. I wanted to run out into the trees, toward freedom, but I needed to get back to Becky. Right now I felt like I couldn't move either way, like I was trapped. I didn't want to listen to Harvard's geometry or Lily's trivia. I didn't care. I—

"Hey," I said, grabbing her hand and looking her in the eye. "What are you doing out here? What about the implant? The pain?"

She smirked. "That's why this is a waste of time." She tried to stand, but I didn't let go, and she fell back to her knees.

"What is going on?"

"It hurts, sure. Kind of like a vibrating headache. But how do we know that my pain threshold is the same as Harvard's? Even if there is something out there, there's no way to tell what direction it's in. And I know my geometry, too—it could be twenty feet away or a hundred. This is pointless." She glanced back again for Harvard, and then stared at me. Her smile was gone. "You need to get out of here."

"I told you already: I'm not leaving without Becky."

"Damn it, Benson," she said. "I've only been here a couple weeks, and I'm already going crazy. I heard about Becky's arm—that's going to take a while to heal, and every day you spend waiting is another chance to be caught."

I peered through the bushes. Harvard wasn't far away,

talking to a guard. He didn't seem to be paying attention to us.

"But I'm helping you," I said. "That was my deal with Birdman. That's what we're doing right now—trying to figure out where these transmitters are."

"This is all Harvard, not Birdman," she said, frustrated. "Birdman's not trying to escape. He's waiting."

"For what?"

Lily shook her head. "Listen, I don't know all the politics of this place, but I've learned there's one subject that no one here talks about: you get too old and they take you away. This whole place exists as a training facility for teenage robots. If you get to be twenty or twenty-one, you don't fit anymore."

"Where do they go?"

Lily shrugged. "No one knows. But Birdman is getting close to the deadline, and he's scared."

"Then he should be trying to escape."

She shook her head. "He thinks they'll take him back underground. That's why he holds the meetings and makes the maps. He thinks that's his best shot."

Harvard was walking toward us.

Lily dropped down into her old hiding place by the tree line, disappearing into the dark shadows.

"It's gone," Harvard said, out of breath, his voice hushed. "I don't know if it was a real one or a camera."

I stood and fought my way through the brush. "I'm going back."

"We made a deal," he said.

My eyes weren't on him as I spoke—I was watching for the deer. "The deal was that I help you if you help Becky. If they find us because I'm out here on some wild-goose chase, how does that help Becky?"

"You're going to have to search for it sooner or later," he said.

"Later." I started across the field, and he had no choice but to follow.

CHAPTER NINE

J ane came to get me the next morning. The sun was already climbing—it was later than I'd thought.

A dozen people were outside. They were all heading to build the new dorms—on Birdman's orders, Jane told me. No one seemed to be protesting, even though I couldn't have been the only one who wished I was still asleep.

Jane insisted I pull the hood of my sweatshirt up to conceal my face as much as possible. She even brought me a knitted scarf that I wrapped around my nose and mouth.

"Did you find anything last night?" she asked as we walked.

I shook my head.

"I didn't think you would."

"It was too dark," I said. "And I wouldn't know what a transmitter looked like if I saw one."

"If they're even out there."

"Well, something's messing up your brain." As soon as I said it, I felt embarrassed. "I mean—"

"It's fine," Jane said. "You're right. There's a transmitter *somewhere.* I just don't believe it's in the forest."

"Where else would it be?"

We entered the shade of the trees along the stream. "I don't know much about science, but I do know that there are better ways to stop us from leaving than putting transmitters around the town."

"Like what?"

"GPS. If they're going to all the trouble to put an implant in our brains, don't you think they'd make sure it could track us no matter where we went?"

She took a step onto a rock dotted with frost. I followed her lead, and we hopped from stone to stone across the stream.

"GPS makes sense," I said, kicking myself that I hadn't thought of it first. It was so much simpler.

"Harvard's just looking for something to do," she said. "We've talked about GPS before, but if that's what it is, there's nothing we can do about it."

I wanted to keep holding her hand. Her skin was warm in the cold morning air, and something about it just felt comfortable, like I wasn't so alone.

Before I could think about what that might mean, Jane stuffed her hands into the front pockets of her cotton jacket, and gave me a quick, uncertain smile.

I could see the others now, all gathered in the field beside the commissary. The stacks of lumber sat uneven on the frozen ground, and several people were already digging the foundation for the new dorm with old, square-ended shovels and heavy picks.

"Don't worry," said a voice behind me. "We have guards out."

I turned to see Mouse.

"I hear you had some problems last night at the tree line?" I couldn't tell whether she was upset with me or with Harvard, but something had ticked her off.

"Just a deer," I said, and turned back to watch the digging.

"Should Benson even be out here right now?" Jane asked.

"We have extra guys at the perimeter," Mouse said. "They'll keep out the animals."

She was gone before Jane could reply.

It didn't make any sense to me, either. Any help I could give building this dorm was only going to be negated by the several guys who had to leave and guard the tree line.

The construction was moving quickly but with precision. These were teenagers, not construction workers, but they seemed to know what they were doing.

"What's the point of this?" I asked, watching the guys dig. "Why make us build the barracks when they could just bring in robot labor? For that matter, why were you milking cows when the school sends food?"

"Keeps us busy," Jane said, and she actually sounded like it didn't bother her. "It's not nearly as strict as at the school—the cows and chickens are here because Maxfield offered and we accepted. We can grow fresh vegetables. But most of the field is for games—soccer and football and whatever else. It's not a terrible place."

"They keep you just happy enough that you won't end up like Dylan."

Someone shouted something, and I looked up to see Shelly staggering in the road. A girl ran to her, grabbed her around the waist, and helped her sit.

"Feedback," Jane said, and tapped her head. "Shelly still has an active dupe."

"And that makes it so she can't stand up?"

Shelly was sitting cross-legged now in the dirt, her face in her hands. She was sobbing, loudly enough that we could hear it thirty feet away.

"Like I said," Jane answered, taking a deep breath and turning away, "if the dupe is feeling a really strong emotion, then it's all you can see. It takes over."

"She's crying," I said stupidly.

"Her dupe's been down in the underground complex for two days," Jane said. Her voice was quiet, somber. "She probably thinks she's going to die."

I sat on the edge of the newly dug trench, next to an enormous mound of gravel, and watched Joel and Walnut mix concrete in an old wheelbarrow. The cold earth under me felt good—my muscles were tired and sore, and I was sweating despite the winter air. I wanted to take the scarf off my face, but didn't dare.

Maybe the reason Birdman wanted me down here was just because he didn't want to shovel out the foundation himself.

"You got a minute?" Without waiting for a response, Shelly sat down beside me.

"Sure. Feeling better?" Despite her earlier episode, she looked completely normal.

"I'm fine," she said. "Totally used to it."

"That makes one of us." Shelly had a Southern accent, something I didn't remember her dupe having. Then again, I didn't know her dupe well.

"You should have seen what this place was like before." She leaned back on her hands and turned her face to the sky as though she were trying to get a tan. "You saw what just happened to me—imagine that happening to everyone, five or ten times a day each."

"Sounds dangerous. What if it happened when you were crossing the stream or something?"

"We have the buddy system. You know when Birdman cuts your arm if you've been alone? That's his paranoid take on a rule I started with the Greens. He uses the buddy system to make sure we don't have dupes infiltrating the town, but I started it to make sure no one falls down the stairs or drowns in the stream because they're getting feedback."

Mouse was watching me from across the field, her face still a massive bruise. I couldn't help but notice that a lot more Greens were working on the barracks than kids from the fort.

I turned to Shelly. I wanted answers. "Someone told me you Greens are cowards."

Shelly's face didn't change noticeably. She picked up a handful of gravel and began tossing the rocks into the dry grass one by one.

"We're not like Birdman," she said, her voice even and emotionless. "Or Mouse or Harvard or Jane." On Jane's name Shelly glanced at me for just an instant before throwing rocks again.

I folded my arms. It was surprising how quickly I'd gone from overheated to freezing. "I've seen what they do with the maps and the lists," I said. "At least they're trying to escape. What do you guys do?"

"We're not cowards," she said with a cold smile. "Who's more paranoid? The people who hide in a fort and slice arms open, or the people who live out in the open?"

"If you're not paranoid, you're stupid." I stood up and offered her a hand. Walnut was pushing the heavy wheelbarrow toward us.

"What do I have to be afraid of? I'm not breaking any rules, and I don't know anyone who's breaking any rules." She took my hand. "Except for the people who are hiding you."

Shelly brushed dirt from her jeans. Walnut heaved the wheelbarrow up, and Joel scraped the cement into the trench.

"So what's your strategy, then?" I asked as they pushed the wheelbarrow back to mix a second batch. "You're just waiting for someone else to solve your problems? Birdman's right—you *are* cowards."

I was goading her, making her mad on purpose. If there was any truth to what Lily said, I didn't want to waste my time with Harvard's crazy midnight hunts and Birdman's useless meetings. I wanted to get out of here.

She paused, and then looked right at me and spoke. "First things first: *we* aren't anything, because there isn't a 'we.' You're not back at the school. There aren't gangs."

"But—"

"No, listen. I want to escape. Tapti wants to escape. Some others do, too." Shelly started pointing around the field at other kids. "But Taylor's suicidal right now. Hog wants to sit and wait it out. Brendan thinks we should negotiate. And Eliana, well . . ."

"What?"

"She's human, but she thinks she's a robot. They've screwed with her brain so much that she doesn't even know who she is. So if you want to show up here without knowing

92

any of us at all and tell me that we're all cowards, then fine. Hooray for you. Go play with Birdman and flirt with Jane and get out of my way."

She gave me a final look and then walked away.

I had no business interrogating anyone. Old habits die hard.

Someone shouted, far away, and then someone else.

The bell at the fort rang. I shot a look at Jane just to see her collapse to the ground. Everyone around me was going limp, dropping violently onto the frozen earth.

I jumped, instinctively running toward the fort. But it was too far. I could hear the sharp buzz of the four-wheelers' engines—they sounded like they were all around me.

One came speeding out of the forest, not following any path, just smashing through the brush and into the open field. I fell to the ground, my face against the cold, slick dirt. I may have looked like one of the other kids from a distance, but I couldn't stay here. They were looking for me.

I crawled on my elbows, not lifting up more than a few inches, and worked my way between two pallets of lumber. In the narrow space I couldn't make out the direction of any of the engines—the sounds were all around me, both near and far.

This wasn't a permanent solution, but I didn't have any other ideas. I was out in the open, fifty yards from the nearest building. Worse, I didn't know which direction I could run—I had no idea where they were. I couldn't see a thing.

I took a deep breath and risked a peek around the edge of the lumber. One of the four-wheelers was racing down the dirt road toward the barn. It passed me without slowing. Iceman was driving.

Without waiting, I darted out from my hiding place and jumped down into the freshly dug trench, landing on the congealing cement. It was still wet, but too dense for me to sink into, and I lay on my back about a foot below ground level. With one hand I tried to scoop from the gravel pile, to create an avalanche that could hide me, but instead of covering myself I only made a lot of noise.

I peered aboveground again. The engines, wherever they were, all sounded like they were idling now. I couldn't see any of them.

I reached for the nearest person—Walnut. "If you can hear me, sorry. I won't enjoy this either." I grabbed his coat by the back of the neck and pulled him toward the trench. He was bigger than me—taller, and his coat was unbuttoned and loose—and when I pulled his body on top of mine it seemed like he hid me pretty well. It was a long shot—my legs could have been sticking out—but it was the best I could do.

I heard voices. Iceman, either talking to himself or to another copy of himself.

This was idiotic. What was I doing out in the open

anyway? If Iceman had just stood at the tree line with binoculars instead of swooping into town he could have easily picked me out. I wasn't going to make this mistake again.

I was going to get Becky and me out of this town. And if Birdman and Shelly were no help, I'd figure it out myself.

It was nearly half an hour before everyone regained consciousness. There were no speeches this time, no announcements that the kids needed to hand us over. Instead, they just searched. I heard doors open and rustling brush. I heard footsteps near me, walking all through the construction site, but they never paused or called anyone over. Eventually the engines revved and disappeared into the forest.

Walnut moved, scrambling up and cussing at me.

"Sorry." I shrugged, clambering out of the slippery cement.

"What if they found you and thought I was hiding you? Did you ever think of that?"

I didn't bother to answer. I was running for the fort before he'd finished. I slipped across the wet rocks of the stream, sinking one foot in the icy water, and darted up the far bank.

I ran the hundred yards to the fort, my soaked shoe heavy and cold, my sweatshirt plastered with wet cement, and I pounded on the old wooden door. No one answered, and I pounded again, yelling for someone to open it.

A few long seconds later I heard the latch, and a guy's face appeared. Since I was alone, he had his box cutter out, ready to check my arm.

He started to ask me what the hurry was, but I grabbed him by the jacket and shoved him out of the way, knocking him to the ground and launching the box cutter from his hand. He yelled something after me, but I ignored him, running for the Basement.

Lily sat on Carrie's bed, a bruise swelling up on her cheek. She took a look at my clothes and smiled.

I breathed a sigh of relief. "Everything okay?"

Lily nodded and scooted the chair over to me so I could climb up into the Basement. Before I could, the door flew open. The sentry was there, and a bigger kid behind him. They both had box cutters out and ready, and the small one looked pissed.

Lily grinned at me. "Didn't let them cut you?"

"You're new here," the sentry said, his arrogance ten times stronger now that he had backup. "So I'll cut you some slack." He grabbed me and drew the razor roughly down my arm. Blood spilled from my skin and dribbled onto the floor.

He spread the skin, checking the bone underneath, and then tossed me a bandage. "Do that again and I'll kill you."

"Oh, yeah," I said, rolling my eyes and climbing back

onto the chair. "It looked like you were really restraining yourself back there while you were lying in the mud."

He took a step toward me, and Lily laughed. "Boys, boys. We're all friends here."

"Tell that to him," the big guy said, and shuffled toward the door.

I ignored them all and pulled myself up into the Basement.

The two vents were closed, and a lantern was burning, filling the room with a warm yellow glow. Becky was still asleep, but she looked more peaceful somehow. I knelt beside her and touched her face—it was damp, but cool. Her fever was gone.

"How is she?"

"She's Becky," Lily said, peering in the opening after me, "which means that this time tomorrow she'll be smiling like an idiot."

Her joking made me tense up, but I tried to push my anger away. "You were here when Iceman came looking?"

"I jumped out when I heard the bell," she said, and touched her bruise. "Landed bad."

"She's okay, though?"

"See for yourself," Lily answered. "It's not in the school's best interest to let people die. They give us good medicine."

I twisted the handle of the lantern, raising the wick and filling the room with bright yellow light.

I moved slowly, peeling back the gauze that wrapped

Becky's bare arm.

With the gauze removed I saw the thin silver patch Jane had laid over Becky's gaping, jagged wound.

I didn't even recognize what I saw underneath.

What had been a tangle of torn and infected muscle was now reassembled into what looked like an almost healthy bicep. I moved the lantern closer, searching for stitches—for anything that explained this—but there was nothing. Her entire upper arm was coated in something clear and thick, and—

No. It couldn't be.

I stared at the wound—the wound that had been infected and festering—and saw new skin growing. Like delicate spiderwebs, tendrils of skin were creeping across the exposed muscle.

CHAPTER TEN

I t's a fort?" Becky asked, peering out the tiny vent onto the courtyard. The sun was just coming up, but she'd been awake for hours.

"Yeah. It was the first Maxfield." I was exhausted, but too happy to sleep. She was almost back to her normal self. It was a miracle.

"That doesn't make any sense," she said, and left the vent to come back and nestle next to me, her good arm against mine. "So they've been kidnapping people for what? A hundred and fifty years?"

"I guess," I said.

"Well, they couldn't have been making robots back then," she said, a smile in her voice. "Would they run on steam power?"

Our situation was ridiculous, but Becky didn't seem concerned at all—just happy and curious. I was sure the worry would set in soon enough. For now, she just seemed glad to be conscious.

"The pipe," she said excitedly. "Steffen Metalworks, 1893. Remember?"

I nodded. An inscription molded into an old pipe coming out of the foundation of the school. She'd shown it to me the night before we left.

"So," she continued, "Maxfield started here, and then around the turn of the century they upgraded to the school. A change in the experiment?"

"That place can hold more people," I said. "And that leaves this town for humans who have dupes."

"There wasn't anything like that school out here back then." Becky had grown up not far from Maxfield—on a ranch in Arizona. She knew a lot more about the history of the Southwest than I did.

I took her hand, and she laced her fingers with mine. "What was there?"

"I studied Arizona history, not New Mexico," she said. "But there would have been Spanish settlements, Pueblo tribes. Navajos and Apaches. There wouldn't—well, there *shouldn't*—have been giant Ivy League–looking private schools with walls around them."

"What do you think it means?"

Becky shrugged, and winced at the movement of her arm. "I wish I knew."

It felt good having her back. She was far from healed, but talking to her—seeing her irrational cheerfulness—filled me with the hope and happiness I hadn't felt since she'd been hurt.

"What do you remember?" I asked. "From the last couple days."

"Not much. A lot of bad dreams." She looked up at me. "When I get sick I have math dreams."

"What's that?"

"I do math in my dreams," Becky said with a small laugh. "I can always tell if I've got a fever, because in my dreams I'll be trying to solve some math problem, and it's impossible. It's just the same thing, over and over, and I try different solutions and nothing ever works."

"That sounds awful."

"It is," she said, and squeezed my hand. "You had it easy out here in the real world."

We sat there quietly for several minutes. I'd already told her all that had happened since we got there.

Her voice was softer now. "You've met everyone here?"

I nodded. "I think so. Unless they're hiding someone else."

Becky rested her head on my shoulder. "So you know who all the robots were back at the school?"

"I do."

She was quiet, waiting. I could only guess how much it would hurt her. She'd been at the school a lot longer than me, and she'd cared more about the other students than I had. I'd been watching out for myself since the day I'd started at Maxfield, but Becky had been watching out for everyone else. She'd helped start the Variants, and then she'd joined the Society because she couldn't handle watching people die.

I swallowed. "There were twenty-two."

She opened her mouth to say something, but stopped.

"By my count, there were sixty-eight of us back at the school when we tried to escape. Twenty-two of those were robots."

Becky didn't make a sound. For a long time, I couldn't even hear her breathe. When she finally spoke, her voice wasn't even as loud as a whisper. "Who?"

I recited the names. I'd made the list, and I'd looked over it a dozen times. I knew them all. Jane, Mouse, Carrie, Mason, and on and on.

She was silently crying by the time I finished.

"It gets worse," I said. "Sixteen people died when we went over the wall—humans. And there's reason to think that at least a few more died after. We'll find out."

I could feel her body tense against mine as she stifled her cries.

"There's a little good news," I said, knowing it wasn't much. "Lily's here. And Jelly and Walnut. And Laura. Anyone who got sent to detention. They weren't killed."

"They came here?"

"The school recycles."

Becky smiled and wiped her eyes. "So, what is there to do for fun around here?"

"A lot of sitting around and talking," I said. "We're building a new barrack. I saw some guys with a Frisbee. Jane milks cows."

She looked up at me. "I assume you've been getting into trouble?"

"Always."

CHAPTER ELEVEN

It wasn't snowing, but the clouds were dark and low. It had to come soon.

The second day of the construction hadn't gone very well. The concrete wasn't setting in this weather, and none of us really knew what to do about it. Shelly had said they'd move forward anyway.

I helped out for a while, but there wasn't much to be done. Some of the supplies were missing—the heavy bolts we needed for attaching the support beams to the piers apparently hadn't come in with the rest of the lumber, and the board count was off. There was an elevator in the commissary—like the supply elevators back at the school—and Shelly left a written message there requesting the missing materials.

I spent most of the day back at the fort, and in the evening Becky finally felt well enough to leave the Basement. The heavy wooden door to the fort was closed and locked, and there were guards on the roof—Mason was up there, and three others. We were safe for the time being.

I sat on the boardwalk, looking across the courtyard at where Becky sat with Carrie, laughing quietly and talking. "You're lucky," Harvard said.

I nodded, my eyes still on Becky. Her arm was in a sling, but I couldn't see it now, hidden under the heavy parka made for someone a foot taller and a hundred and fifty pounds heavier.

"If you can call this luck," Birdman said, leaning forward to warm his hands over the campfire that we'd built on the ground. "So she's getting better. Big deal."

"She almost died," Jane said.

Birdman shrugged and shoved his warmed hands inside his pockets. "Great. Now she can get caught and have an implant jammed into her head. Or she can get killed trying to escape."

I couldn't say the same thoughts hadn't been going through my head, but it still hurt to hear them out loud.

"Or they'll escape." Jane's tone wasn't very convincing.

"We will," I said. "That's what we're here for."

Becky glanced over and smiled.

I didn't turn my head as I spoke. "I have a question." Becky was getting better, and an escape attempt seemed more of a certainty. It was time to figure out whether Lily had been right.

"There are always new people showing up at the school, right? And more people keep trickling in here. And it's been going on a long time. So why aren't there any adults here?"

Harvard turned to me, excited. "Here's my theory. Someone is trying to create hyperrealistic androids, right? Well, we've speculated on a million reasons for them to do that, but no one can think of any reason they'd only want hyperrealistic androids of *teenagers*. I mean, can you?"

The thought had never really crossed my mind.

"Maybe they . . . I don't know," I stammered. I couldn't think of a reason. "Create an army of robot teenagers and release them on the population because no one would suspect kids?"

Birdman laughed at the suggestion.

"That's part of my theory, though," Harvard said. "We know they're making androids of teenagers, and we know that doesn't make sense, so I think we can assume this isn't the only android training facility."

"What do you mean?"

Harvard started to answer, but Birdman talked over him. "It means that we're screwed."

"Depends on how you look at it," Jane said, staring at the fire.

Harvard nodded. "When you get too old, they take you away. It's happened a dozen times since I've been here."

"Really?" I said. "That's weird. Maybe they just take them away to kill them."

Harvard scoffed. "You're still stuck in the mind-set that

this place is some evil torture chamber. No, I think they have to have a reason for what they're doing. We've seen them kill plenty of people here—you saw them kill Dylan—so if they just killed adults, then why wouldn't they do it here? No, they take adults away. I think it's to another training facility. For adults."

"So it never ends."

"That's bad and good," Jane said. She flicked a sliver of wood into the fire and watched it burn. "We don't get out of here. But we don't die, either."

Birdman stood up and turned his back to the fire to warm himself. "And what's so bad about this place?"

I shook my head. "I've heard that crap before."

Birdman's response was sharp and fast, like he'd been waiting for me. "It's time you listen to it. You're not going to lead a rebellion here."

"I thought the whole reason I'm here is to help you escape."

Birdman looked at Harvard, who answered in his usual excited tone. "We have a lot of things we want you to do— like look for the transmitters—but most important, we want *you* to escape. It's not that we don't want to get out of here. We just don't want to put our necks on the chopping block."

"So you're putting mine."

It was Birdman who answered. "We already took our risk by hiding you here." He pointed to Becky. "And it looks like we fulfilled our part of the bargain. Now we want you to escape so you can get us out of here."

"It'll still be a while before she can travel," I said.

"You don't have to leave yet," Jane said quickly.

I looked at her, but she refused to meet my eyes.

Back at Maxfield, I'd thought she'd been giving up, that she was scared. Now I realized it was because the real Jane, the Jane here at the fort who was giving that android her emotions, was resigned. She'd rather face the unknown of adulthood in another prison than risk her life in an escape.

Lily was right. No one was trying to escape. Jane had given up; Harvard was crazy; Birdman was only planning for when he got too old and had to leave.

I'd been wasting my time.

We sat in awkward silence for several minutes watching the flames flicker and pop, leaving a trail of sparks winding up toward the dimming sky. I didn't think I'd ever sat around a campfire before. Back in Pittsburgh we'd occasionally started a fire in a metal trash can in the winter, but this was the closest I'd ever come to camping.

"Want to know how it works?" Harvard said, breaking the silence and changing the subject.

"How what works?" I glanced at Birdman and he rolled his eyes.

"How Maxfield works," Harvard said.

That surprised me. "You know?"

Birdman answered, his voice annoyed and tired. "He guesses."

"I hypothesize," Harvard corrected. "So, here's the sixty-four-thousand-dollar question."

Jane laughed a little, but it wasn't annoyed, like Birdman. It almost sounded relieved. "One thing you'll have to get used to. Every conversation with Harvard ends up with this question."

"Because it's the most important thing we need to figure out," he said.

"Why we're here?" I guessed.

"No, no, no! We know why we're here. We're here so they can test the androids. We're here because of the neural link, and you guys at the school are props."

"Props?"

"Yeah," Harvard said, seeming to ignore the callousness of his statement. "Maxfield needs something for their robots to interact with. One of the big goals, I assume, is to fool the humans at the school."

Birdman shot me a cruel look and winked. "You and Jane know something about that, right?"

Jane shot him a quick look, then stood and walked away.

"No, the question isn't why we're here," Harvard said. "That's been answered. The question is: who is Maxfield?"

I shrugged.

"Well," he said, "what do we know about them? Three big

things. First, we know they started out here with this fort, and we know this fort is old—at least a hundred and fifty years."

"You assume," Birdman said.

"These are all assumptions," he said, unfazed. "We know that at some point they expanded out of the fort. Benson, you told me about the pipe that Becky found—that school is old. Maxfield has been here a long time."

He stood up, gesturing while he talked. "Second, this level of technology is ridiculous. Just think of all the crazy things they had to figure out. They had to build a robot that, structurally, was a perfect match for a human. Then they had to figure out the artificial intelligence—not only to make the robot act like a human, but to think that it's human, that it's real."

I nodded. "And they had to make them look real."

"Yes!" he said, pointing at me. "And it's more than just looking real—the dupes have real skin. They bleed. They eat and sleep and breathe and think. They're more than just robots that look human—they're like artificial humans. How does that work?"

Birdman tapped on his forehead. "And there's the implant."

Harvard spun to face him. "The implant is crazy. And what about a power source? What's keeping those dupes running for years? They don't plug themselves in at night."

"I get it," I said. "They're high-tech."

"They're more than high-tech," Harvard exclaimed.

"They're *impossibly* high-tech."

Birdman shook his head and sighed. "This is where you start taking things with a grain of salt."

Harvard was indignant. "What?"

"You're smart," Birdman said with a laugh. "But the last grade you completed was what? Eighth?"

"Ninth," he said. "And that doesn't matter. You don't have to go to college to know that a jet is more high-tech than a biplane."

"What's the third thing?" I asked. "They've been here a long time, they're high-tech, and what's number three?"

"Money," Birdman said, standing up. He kicked one of the logs, rolling it toward the center of the fire. "They built this place and the school, and they own all this land, and they feed us all, and they pay for whatever makes the androids work. They have a lot of money."

"So what does this tell you?" Harvard asked. I could tell he'd rather I ask him to enlighten me, but I wanted to take a guess.

"The technology doesn't matter," I said, "because of the money. Anyone with the money could have the technology."

Harvard frowned. "No, the technology's still important, because it's so impossible."

Birdman smiled. "If you'd never seen that jet, you'd think it was impossible, too. Just because you don't understand it doesn't mean it's impossible."

"The time is what's most important," I said. "Because we know that whoever is behind this isn't a single person. It's a group. Anybody here at the beginning would be long dead by now."

Harvard looked like he still wanted to talk about the technology, but he grudgingly nodded. "Right. We're not talking mad scientist, or crazy rich guy. We're talking about an organization."

"Government," Birdman said. "Has to be."

"That's my guess," Harvard said. "This is Area 51 a hundred years before Area 51. Government testing."

Birdman kicked at the fire again, angrier. "It should be pretty obvious. This is a fort. U.S. military. And who else would be able to keep this huge area a secret? Why doesn't the forest service come through here once in a while?"

He was right. It should have been pretty obvious. I wasn't a historian, but I couldn't think of a group that could fit. Other ideas ran through my head—the Masons or the Illuminati or a dozen other conspiracies—but that stuff was only in the movies. Then again, so were androids.

"It still doesn't make sense," I said.

Birdman turned to leave. "Screw sense. C'mon, Harvard."

Before they left, Birdman looked at me. "Here's *my* most important question: If it is the government, do you think we'll ever get help? Even if we escape?"

He didn't wait for an answer, but strode off to the meeting room, Harvard a few steps behind him.

I felt frozen. Stuck. Helpless. I'd led too many people to their deaths, and I'd stood idly by while terrible people hurt the innocent. But what else was I supposed to do? Turn myself in? Live here until I got too old, and then be hauled away to an unknown fate? What if they just killed us all?

I looked up at the roof, at the guards who stood watch for animals and androids. They spent endless hours worrying about security. Maybe they could help me sort this out. And it was about time I finally talked to Mason.

There was a ladder, hand-built and rickety, in the corner of the fort for the guards to get up on the roof. I made sure my scarf was in place, and then climbed up.

There were four guys up there, but I knew only one of them.

"Hey, Mason."

He looked over at me, quiet and nervous, and then turned back to scanning the fields around us. It was dark, but the snow on the ground highlighted every rock and tree. There was a man walking slowly around the perimeter.

I instinctively ducked, though he was too far and it was too dark for him to recognize me.

"How long has he been out there?"

"Twenty minutes."

"You didn't ring the warning bell?"

"Deer are out there almost every night," he said. "Today it's Iceman. But they're all robots."

We stood in silence and watched.

"What are punishments like here?" I asked, staring at the shadowy figure in the distance. He was in no hurry, just wandering slowly along the tree line.

"You don't change," he said, with a quiet chuckle.

"I don't blame you," I said, even though I had to force the words out. "For what happened to Becky."

He didn't answer. It was his dupe that attacked her, after he'd popped. He wasn't in control—it wasn't even his emotions.

"Punishments aren't as bad as at the school," he finally said, changing the subject. "We're too valuable. They have to keep us happy. You saw what happened to Dylan."

"Then I'm going to kill that guy."

He laughed, too loud. "The hell you are."

"Haven't you ever wanted to see what's inside one of those things?"

"Punishments here aren't bad for *us*," he said, emphasizing the last word. "We are important. You're not. You don't have a dupe, and you're a pain in Maxfield's butt."

I didn't care. "Do you have a weapon?"

"No."

I didn't believe him. One of the other guards was very obviously carrying a baseball bat, and another had a claw

114

hammer hanging from his hand.

"Mason," I said, "I don't care about what your dupe did. That wasn't you. But this is you, and I need help."

"You don't get it," he said, suddenly looking older, tougher, as I looked into his face. "It didn't work. Sixty people tried and only two made it past the fence. What makes you think you can go another fifty miles by yourself?"

"I've killed other robots. It's not impossible."

I walked to the outside wall of the fort and looked down at the snow twelve feet below. He followed me. "Becky's getting better," I said. "And the deal was, they take care of Becky and I help you escape."

"You're not doing this for Becky," Mason said coldly. "You're doing it for you."

I turned back to give him one final look. "You're not the same Mason I knew back at the school," I said. "I get that. And I'm not the same Benson. I've changed."

With that, I swung a leg over the low wall, and then jumped down to the frozen ground outside the fort.

Shelly answered the door of her barrack, wearing the same pajamas she'd had on the other night. I pulled down my scarf long enough for her to recognize who I was. She looked surprised to see me.

"Can I come in?" I asked quietly, looking past her at the room of curious faces. "We need to talk—privately."

She nodded, stepping aside to let me in. She closed the door behind me, and then motioned for the rest of the room to get back to whatever they'd been doing.

"Lily told me something," I whispered. "And I didn't believe it until now."

"That Birdman's full of crap?"

"Pretty much."

"I don't trust you, Benson," she said, her voice firm.

"I can cut my arm for you."

She shook her head. "It's not that. You're human. You're courageous. And you're stupid and impatient."

I paused, surprised. That wasn't what I'd expected.

"I think you're trying to escape," I said.

"What makes you say that?"

"Because you don't act like you've given up."

"That's not a lot of evidence."

"I think it's true, and I want in," I said, "but that's not what I came to see you about. I just need your help."

She stared at me for a long time. She looked old for her age, tired and strong.

"What?"

"I need a new coat, one that no one will recognize, preferably white. I'd love a ski mask." I pointed to the woodpile next to the fireplace. "And I want that hatchet."

She smiled, uncertain.

"I'm not going to murder Birdman."

Shelly laughed quietly. "Wait here."

The fort was silent when I got back, but my breath was heaving, and my heart was pounding out of my chest. They checked my arm when I came in—I was almost getting used to that by now—and I jogged to Harvard's room, pounding on his door. After a moment he answered. His grogginess dissolved instantly when he saw the blood on my coat.

I panted for air. "How long does it take Maxfield to get here when there's trouble?"

"About twenty minutes," he said, already pulling on his shoes. "Depends on how mad they are."

"Then you have about eighteen minutes to dissect Iceman. He's sitting on the road in front of the fort."

A grin broke across his face, and he was out of his room in an instant, banging on Birdman's door but not waiting for an answer before he ran to the heavy fort door and out into the road.

I was exhausted, frozen to the bone. It hadn't been a hard fight, but I'd spent an hour facedown in the snow, stalking him. When I finally got close enough, it had taken only two hits—one aimed for his neck, and then another flailing, desperate blow that smashed through his metal spine.

He'd never even seen me. It was over too fast for him to turn around.

Maxfield would be here soon. I jogged back to Carrie's room. She didn't stir when I entered, or when I slid a chair across the rough wooden floor to the wall. I lifted the cloth drawing, removed the panel, and climbed in.

Becky was asleep, the short lantern wick just barely holding a trickle of flame.

I took off my shoes and pulled my black Steelers sweatshirt back on. It was filthy and crusted from my time in the cement, but it was dry now, and warm.

I lay down next to her. The room was too narrow for me to avoid touching her, not that I wanted to avoid it. I wanted to hug her, and hold her, and tell her what happened.

"Hey, Bense," she whispered sleepily.

"Hey, Becky."

I did something, Becky. We're in danger. I wanted to say it, but all I did was blow out the lantern.

Lily had to be right. The Greens were the fighters, not Birdman. I needed to find out for sure.

She reached over with her good hand and touched my arm. "How are things?"

"I don't know."

A few minutes later the warning bell rang. I heard the outer door creak open and then slam shut and lock. A moment later, the roar of the truck engine filled the night air.

I'd put people in danger. But maybe it would help. Maybe Harvard would learn something.

I'd definitely learned something. I needed Shelly more than I needed Birdman.

I woke in the morning to the sound of voices. They weren't shouting, or laughing, or yelling. They were just talking. I sat up, but Becky was faster, peeking out the vent toward the courtyard.

"Are they having another meeting?" I asked.

She shrugged and turned back to me. "I don't see anything."

I moved to the other vent.

"Oh, Becky . . ."

Chapter Twelve

Becky and I hadn't made it five steps out of Carrie's room before Birdman shouted at us.

"Get back inside," he snapped, striding across the courtyard to me.

"They're here," I said, still moving toward the door.

"Dammit, get back in your hole," he said. "We haven't checked them yet. Half of 'em could be dupes for all we know. And don't think Maxfield's not going to double security after your stunt last night."

Becky looked at me. We both knew he was right, but from the look on her face I almost thought she couldn't survive the wait.

"How long will it take?"

He started for the door. "As long as it takes. And I'm sure as hell not bringing them all in here. This fort is secure, and I don't bring anyone in that I don't trust." He shook his head. "Except you, I guess."

Becky stood in the cold morning air, staring at the gate, hopeful and scared.

She didn't look guilty—that was all me. I'd led them to their deaths, not her. She was probably thinking more about them now, about how they'd suffered and how she could help them. I was thinking about how I needed to beg for forgiveness.

More people in the fort were spilling out of their rooms now, eager to greet their friends they'd never actually met.

I put my arm around Becky's waist and pulled her toward me.

"I have to see them," she said, hardly above a whisper.

"We will," I said. "We just need to be safe."

Our eyes locked for several seconds before she nodded and we walked back to Carrie's room.

Carrie was anxiously brushing her hair, trying to see herself in the broken shard of a mirror she kept on her table. She turned to look at us, nervous and embarrassed.

"You look beautiful," Becky said, breaking into a smile.

"He's here," she said. "I saw him through the window."

I'd seen Curtis, too, actually walking on his injured leg. Just two days ago they were saying he might lose it, but he was walking without a crutch. There was a noticeable limp, but that was hardly something to complain about. Whatever advanced medicine the school had supplied us with that was healing Becky's arm must have also saved Curtis's leg.

"Is this a new shirt?" Becky asked, touching the thin

yellow linen that was the cleanest fabric I'd seen since getting here.

"I've been saving it. I wanted to look nice."

Becky turned Carrie around and looked at her. "He's going to love you."

Carrie's face contorted for a moment, like she was going to break down and sob, but she pulled it back and took a deep breath.

"Go get him," Becky said.

Carrie nodded and left, leaving her coat on the bed.

"Please, Curtis," Becky whispered. "Don't freak out."

I pulled Becky to me and held her tight.

We watched out the window as the disheveled group gathered. Becky had her journal and was quickly scribbling a list of everyone she'd seen. Last we'd heard, sixteen had died at the fence. We knew Hector had been killed back at the school. What we hadn't been prepared for was how small the group of survivors was.

Thirty-three. When I'd gotten to the school, there were seventy-two. Sure, many of those had turned out to be androids, but that didn't do much to make me feel better. Seeing the thirty-four of them here, rounded up in a confused circle as the people in the town spoke to them, made my stomach turn. Half the school was gone.

Birdman stood in front of them and talked for a while.

More than once I saw him point to his head. He was explaining. No one was freaking out, not like I was expecting. Some were crying, some were hugging each other, but they weren't scared or enraged—they were tired and defeated.

I could see Carrie standing away from the crowd, shivering in her new short-sleeved shirt. Curtis was staring at her, stony faced.

He thought she'd betrayed him. Her dupe had popped, and the robot Carrie had taken the gun from Curtis and she'd killed Oakland. It wasn't like me and Jane. Jane had broken my heart and messed with my brain, but I'd known her for only a few short weeks. Carrie and Curtis loved and trusted each other, and maybe this very moment was the first time he realized she wasn't just a robot—that there was a real Carrie. And Carrie—the real Carrie—was in love with him.

Birdman finished his speech and directed them away from our view, off toward the Greens.

"Twenty Society," Becky said, setting her journal down. Her voice was pained. "Seven from Havoc. Six from the V's. That's all that's left."

"A lot of them were dupes," I said. "I mean, Carrie and Mason and Shelly and all the others."

Becky sighed and stood up, moving away from the window. "That's the problem."

"What?"

"Look at the names," she said, gesturing to her journal and walking to the door. "Almost all of the dupes were from Havoc and Variants."

"So what?" If anything, that meant that more of her friends were just who they thought they were.

"*We* had the security contracts—the Society," she said, staring out at the empty courtyard. "We were running the school, and guarding the walls, and enforcing the rules. And it was all voluntary." She turned her head, looking at me over her shoulder. "When I found out about the androids, I'd almost hoped . . ."

She didn't finish. She didn't have to.

Isaiah had been out there, in the group of tired survivors.

Not that it mattered. Even the dupes got their personality from a human. We couldn't blame anything we'd done to each other on androids. It was all us. We'd fought and killed each other, and it was all us.

I built a fire in the pit, and Becky and I sat together, a blanket draped around our shoulders. It was snowing again, tiny crystal flakes that weren't sticking to anything but that seemed to make everything colder and sharper. We were almost the only ones left in the fort—everyone else was out talking to the new arrivals.

With all that was going on, I hadn't heard anything about the dissection of Iceman. I needed to talk to Harvard when things calmed down.

The heavy door squeaked, and Birdman entered the fort, Mouse and Harvard in tow. Becky was on her feet instantly.

"They're all clean," he said, pointing to us. "Come with me."

He disappeared into his room for a minute and then came back with an armful of old cloth. We all followed him to the meeting room.

"You haven't been here for a new arrival," he said. "We have procedures we usually go through. And now we've got a ton to process."

He laid the cloth out on the floor of the meeting room. I recognized some of it as what he'd written on during our last group meeting, but there was a lot more here—drawings and floor plans and lists.

"We keep track of what's going on in that underground complex," Birdman said, pointing to what looked like an amazingly detailed floor plan. "Like I was telling you yesterday—one day they're going to take us out of here, and I want to know what I'm dealing with."

Harvard peeked out one of the windows, and then turned back to us. "We know you guys want to talk to everyone you knew at the school, and we kind of want to see what they have to say to you. Maybe they'll tell you something they're not telling us."

"Like what?"

"I don't know," he said. "We'll find out."

There were six of us seated in the room—me and Becky, Birdman, Harvard, Mouse, and Shelly. She'd been added at the last minute, when the Greens figured out what was going on. Our six chairs faced three empty ones. It looked like an inquisition.

Most of the town was at the windows, trying to peek or listen, but Birdman was fiercely regulating the fort, and no one was allowed in without his permission. The thick curtains were pulled down, and the only light in the room came from the few dim lanterns. The town was on lockdown.

Birdman motioned to the kid at the door. "Bring in the first group."

I took Becky's hand, and after a moment she had to make me let go—I didn't realize how hard I was squeezing.

Isaiah was the first one in. His head was held high, but it was an imitation of the pious confidence he'd always had at the school. There was fear in his eyes.

He took a seat on the bench opposite us and stared straight ahead, a prisoner.

Behind him was Skiver, Oakland's right-hand man before he was shot. He stopped just inside the door, staring at Mouse. He wasn't scared—not like Isaiah—but something was going on in his head.

"Sit down," Mouse said. It was an order, but there was no edge to her voice. It hardly sounded like her at all.

The third to enter was Gabby. Becky stood up, wanting to run to her, but Birdman held up a hand forbidding it.

We'd thought Gabby was dead or dying. The last I'd seen of her, she was lying on the ground, covered in blood and screaming. But even though there was obvious pain in her face as she crossed the room to the bench, she was walking and breathing and alive.

Birdman was slouched a little in his chair, the kind of casual stance of someone who knew he was in complete control. His calm was a show. It was a threat.

"You're representatives of the three gangs at the school," he said. "And—"

Gabby immediately protested. "I wasn't in charge. You want Curtis."

"Neither was Skiver," Birdman said flatly. "This isn't a leadership meeting."

Gabby looked to me for help, but I just shrugged. I didn't know what Birdman wanted. I didn't care, either. Becky and I were leaving. I needed to talk to Harvard about the dissection, and I needed to see what help Shelly could offer, but then we were leaving.

"You're here now," Birdman continued. "I need to know everything you know. I need to know who is trustworthy and who could be working for the other side."

Gabby's face contorted. "Working for the other side? What's that supposed to mean?"

"Maxfield has tried to bribe students in the past. We checked to make sure that you're not duplicates—androids—but we need to know if Maxfield gave someone something in exchange for spying on us."

"No one here would spy," Gabby said, but as soon as the words were out of her mouth a sudden look of understanding appeared on her face, and for just an instant she glanced at Isaiah.

If Birdman caught it, he didn't react.

"We need information," he continued, gesturing to the cloth maps. "We're going to talk to everyone, but we're going to start with you."

Gabby protested again, and Birdman ignored her.

"Tell me what happened after the fence," Birdman ordered.

There was a pause for a moment, and then Skiver spoke. He pointed at me and Becky. "After they abandoned us, there was—"

"We did not abandon you," I snapped.

"Ran away when people started dying?" he said. "What do you call that?"

"We were trying to get help," I said, anger boiling up inside of me.

"That was days ago," he said. "And you've made it all the way here? What is that? A quarter mile a day? So you'll make it to the highway sometime next summer?"

"We had to stop," I said, and gestured to Becky's arm. "She was going to die."

"Going to die?" Skiver said, almost laughing. "Do you know how many people died at the fence? Do you know how many died back at the school?" He turned to Gabby. "Show him what they did to you."

Gabby was obviously uncomfortable.

"Show them," Skiver screamed, his eyes crazed, and grabbed at her shirt.

She pulled away and shot us all a dark look. Slowly, she pulled up her shirt to show us her stomach, wrapped completely in white gauze. "I don't know what they did," she said. "I was in surgery longer than all the others, even longer than Curtis."

"Artificial organs," Isaiah said, speaking for the first time.

Gabby lowered her shirt and turned her face away from us.

"She was the worst of them," Isaiah said, harsh judgment in his eyes as he stared back at me. "The worst of the survivors. The students who helped her said they could see she was going to die—it doesn't take a doctor to recognize torn intestines and mangled organs."

"I'm okay," she said, but her words seemed to enrage Isaiah.

"You could have died, like the others. Like Oakland,

and Hector, and Rosa. And for what? So that Benson Fisher could get to this town." He pointed at me, his hand shaking with anger. "This is your fault. You stirred everyone up. You got them mad. You led them to the fence."

I wanted to stand up and break his jaw.

But I couldn't. It was all true. They were dead, and it was because of me.

"Stop it, Isaiah," Becky said, her voice stronger than it had been since we'd left the school.

"I tried to stop you," he continued, ignoring her. "I tried to make you understand what we needed to do to survive, but you just couldn't let it go. You had to be a tough guy and fight and run, and look what it got you.

"And you," he continued, turning to Becky, a cruel smile creeping onto his tired face. "You knew what happened to people who run. Don't you think that people followed Benson because they saw you join him? People trusted you, Becky, and you led them to their deaths."

She stood, and I thought for a moment she was going to storm out. Her chest rose and fell with painful, angry breaths.

Isaiah grinned. He opened his mouth to speak, but she didn't let him.

"You're wrong," she said. Her voice was quiet but firm, and it rose with intensity as she spoke. "Every single person who followed you had a death sentence the moment they joined the Society. If they'd listened to you, they'd sit in that school until they died or got hauled here. And then they'd sit here until they died or got hauled somewhere else. People got killed during the escape, but at least they died fighting."

He barked back, spreading his arms wide. "Are you seriously saying that everyone in this room would be better off dead?"

"Everyone there knew what they were getting themselves into," she yelled. "They went willingly."

"They thought he"—Isaiah jabbed a finger at me—"had a plan."

Gabby was on her feet now, her hand clutching her stomach as she shouted. There were calls from the windows, too, from behind the curtains, and more bodies pressed in at the door. Becky's face was pained and straining, but she was closer to Isaiah now, her voice drowned out by the chaos.

I stood and reached for her arm, but she ignored me and kept on yelling.

Birdman clapped his hands and called the room to order. No one paid any attention. It was only then that I noticed that the other leaders—Harvard, Mouse, and Shelly—were quietly staying out of things.

Birdman stomped his feet and clapped his hands once more. "Quiet," he bellowed.

Becky pulled away from me and slapped Isaiah. For a moment he reeled back, only to come up fighting. He threw a punch and I stepped in front of it, his fist deflecting off my shoulder.

There was a tremendous crash.

"Shut up," Birdman yelled again, standing over a long wooden bench he'd just toppled. "Shut the hell up, all of you."

I wanted to hit Isaiah—just one punch to punish him for everything he'd done. But it wouldn't be enough. It couldn't ever be enough.

Birdman seethed. Isaiah glared back, his face reddening from the slap.

"You were the big man at the school," Birdman said, motionless.

Isaiah was standing firm, but silent.

"I don't know if you've figured out how this place works. But we can see what's going on inside people's heads." He reached out with one arm and touched Shelly's hair. She shook his hand away. "Shelly was part of your gang. Every time her dupe saw something important over there, Shelly saw it here."

Isaiah's voice shook. "I kept the peace."

Someone at a window swore, and Mouse laughed. Shelly looked uncomfortable, like she didn't want to be mentioned—or even to be in the room.

Birdman bent and whispered something to Harvard, who nodded and pushed his way out the door.

"You kept the peace," Birdman said, crossing his muscular arms and taking a step toward Isaiah.

"If you saw what was going on then you know about the war," Isaiah said. "I led the truce. I fought for peace."

Skiver scoffed and started to speak, but Birdman gestured for him to be quiet. The wave of his hand was hardly noticeable, but there was something about it so menacing and powerful that the color drained from Skiver's face.

"I think the key word there," Birdman said, "is that you *fought* for peace. You and your boys killed people until the rest were too afraid to fight anymore. That's peace?"

"I didn't—" Isaiah said, and then stammered. He broke eye contact with Birdman, and his eyes shot all around the room looking for help. All he found was anger and fear.

"We saw what happened," Birdman said, taking another step toward Isaiah. "We know who you talked to. We know the orders you gave."

"I was stopping the war."

Birdman was now directly in front of Isaiah, inches from his face. Harvard appeared at the door, pulling Jane by the arm.

My stomach dropped. I guessed what was coming next.

She resisted Harvard, straining against his tight grasp, but she didn't fight him. She must have known there was no way to stop it.

Birdman broke into a fake smile. "Hey! Jane's here.

Isaiah, you remember Jane, right?"

Isaiah's head hung down, his face to the floor.

"Look at her," Birdman said.

Jane's eyes met mine for an instant.

"Look at her!" Birdman grabbed Isaiah's face with one hand, and his shoulder with the other. Isaiah fell to his knees and stared, terrified, up at Jane.

No one moved.

Birdman's voice was quiet again. "Dylan lived here until a couple days ago. He told us how you pulled him aside at the dance, after Jane made a toast to Lily. He told us what you ordered him and Laura to do."

Isaiah moaned—weak and soft, like an animal.

"Laura's already been on trial. She's not here right now, because she's spent the last few weeks in chains. And she was only the pawn. Now we have the king."

Birdman's mouth was inches from Isaiah's ear, but I could hear every word in the dead silence of the room.

And now Birdman was grabbing Jane, shoving her down so she was eye level with Isaiah.

I stepped forward and Harvard shot me a look of frightened caution.

"Say you're sorry," Birdman said, a hand on each of their shoulders as he spit at Isaiah. "Tell her what you ordered, you damn murdering bastard, and look her in the eye and tell her you're sorry."

Jane pulled away, but Birdman's grip was iron. She winced as his fingers dug deeper.

"Birdman," I said. The name came out in a dry whisper.

"Say it," Birdman barked. "Tell her."

Harvard motioned for me to step back, but I couldn't. This wasn't right. It wasn't even clear who Birdman was punishing anymore—Isaiah or Jane.

"Let her up," I said.

Jane's eyes met mine again, and there was nothing but fear in them.

"Birdman—"

And then they were both thrown to the ground and Birdman was in my face, screaming.

"Hey," I said, backing up, hands raised. "I'm not looking for a fight."

"You're a pansy-ass coward," he yelled. "You use your traitor girlfriend as an excuse to hide in a hole."

"Traitor?"

Becky pulled on my arm. "Don't."

Birdman threw his arm back and pointed at Isaiah, who was slowly picking himself up off the floor. "She worked for him! For a year! Because she was a coward, just like you."

Becky jumped in between us. "Stop it! Yes, I was scared."

"Becky . . ."

She looked me in the eye, her expression hurt and desperate. "I was scared. I'm still scared."

We stared at each other. She hadn't done it because she was scared—she'd done it because, unlike everyone else at that school, she was genuinely concerned about other people. She didn't want anyone to get hurt. She'd seen too much death. It wasn't fear that made her join the Society. It was courage.

I should have said that, but Birdman was looking at me over her shoulder, derision in his eyes. All I wanted to do was fight.

I took a step to get around Becky, and Birdman shoved her toward me.

She screamed, first from fear and then from pain as I caught her, and her injured arm slammed into my chest.

"You can go to hell," I shouted over her shoulder, cradling her shaking body. She gasped, gulping at the air as she fought the pain.

He turned away. "Back to business."

Birdman slumped down into his chair and gestured toward the door. Harvard hurried away.

"Mouse," Birdman ordered, tossing her a roll of cloth that had been lying beside his chair. "Tell the man what he's won."

Isaiah stood alone against the wall. Jane was gone—slipped out of the room when I wasn't watching. Shelly was gone, too.

Mouse smiled and took a long breath. Whatever she was

about to say, she took great pleasure in it. The cloth was laid out on her lap, but she wasn't reading from it. She knew what was there without looking.

"Isaiah. You ran the Society for a year. Before that, you led the most brutal gang at the school."

"I—"

"Shut up and listen," Birdman whispered, sharp and cold.

"We know about four murders," Mouse continued. "Three during the war, and Jane."

"Jane didn't die," Isaiah said. "She was a robot."

Birdman leaned forward, but his voice was steady and controlled. "Shut your damn mouth or I'm going to rip your tongue out."

"She didn't . . ." Isaiah's voice trailed off.

Mouse continued, tapping the cloth. "Four that we know of, but several murders weren't accounted for. There are also those you sent to detention."

She paused, like she was waiting for him to protest, but he didn't. He could feel what was coming.

I was worried that *I* knew what was coming. They couldn't do this.

Mouse smiled at him—a twisted, evil smile, like she was slowly pulling the wings off a fly. "Do you need me to give you that number, or do you remember them?"

Isaiah's face was totally white now, and he looked younger

than he was, and thin and fragile. He wasn't arguing; he was pleading. "What was I supposed to do? We had the security contract."

Birdman laughed.

"Eight," Mouse said. "You sent eight to detention."

"But they got sent here, right? They didn't die in detention."

Harvard reappeared at the door. "They don't all die, no," he said. "Only two of them did. They must have fought back, or the implant didn't take, or—"

Mouse sneered. "You didn't have any idea what happened in detention, and you didn't care—death, torture, whatever. You just did what Maxfield told you to do."

Birdman motioned for them both to be quiet, and then he stood.

"Isaiah," he said. "I'm not you. I don't lead a gang. I'm not working for the school, and I don't have any contracts to fill. Instead, I run this fort, and I keep my people safe."

Tears began to flow down Isaiah's face. "Just let me go."

Mouse laughed again, and Birdman smiled. "That's actually exactly what I had in mind."

Becky shuddered. We couldn't do anything but watch.

"So," Birdman said, motioning to Harvard. "You can live down at the Greens, and I'll see you in the commissary, and we can tell stories about the good old days."

Isaiah almost looked like he believed it.

"Even better," Birdman said, looking toward the door. "I have a peace offering." A few more people started filing into the room. I knew two of them. Walnut and Jelly.

Oh, no.

Isaiah began to convulse, sobbing loudly and falling to his knees.

"I've arranged an escort for you," Birdman said.

Walnut and Jelly had been sent to detention. I'd watched Walnut dragged on his back down the floor of the school, Isaiah leading the procession of attackers. The six of them standing in the room looked like they were eager for payback.

"You can't do this," I said.

"Do what?" Birdman asked innocently.

People at the windows began shouting, some calling for Isaiah's blood and others screaming for mercy.

"Mouse," I said. "Aren't you better than this?"

She smiled and raised her hands. "I'm not doing anything."

"Come on," I protested. "Walnut—you can't."

He stared back at me from across the room. He didn't say a word. He didn't have to.

"Isaiah," Becky said, tears on her face. "I'm sorry."

He looked at her. There was no snide comment. No "I

hope you're happy." No accusations of hypocrisy. Only fear.

Walnut stepped forward, one of the hammers from the work site tight in his fist. He stared down at Isaiah.

"You gonna walk, or do we need to carry you?"

CHAPTER THIRTEEN

Becky and I were the only ones left in the room, and neither of us spoke. Screams and laughter echoed around the heavy adobe walls, and arms reached through the narrow windows as those outside fought to get in. Mouse and Harvard had taken the lanterns with them when they'd gone, leaving the two of us in darkness.

I didn't want to go outside. I couldn't stop them, and I didn't want to watch anyone—even Isaiah—being beaten to death.

Becky's jaw was clamped shut, her teeth gritted against the pain in her arm.

Someone called from a window, "Open the fort! They're killing him."

"There's nothing I can do," I said, too quiet for them to hear. There were too many of them. They were armed.

"Benson!" another voice shouted. "Help him!"

"I can't!" I shouted, standing up now. "There's nothing I can do."

Something clattered across the floor. It was too dark to see what.

Becky grabbed my leg, and I crouched back down next to her. Blood was oozing through her shirt. Her arm had been healing rapidly, but her fall had reinjured the muscle.

She fought against the pain. "We have to try."

"No."

Something else was flung into the room, smacking into the far adobe wall and knocking plaster to the floor.

I put my arm around her shoulders to coax her up, but Becky didn't budge. It wasn't stubbornness—it was pain.

"Come on," I said.

"I'm okay," she said, more to herself than to me. "I'll be okay."

The noise at the windows subsided for a moment, and then I heard the yells and grunts of a fight. The entire town had exploded. Those still loyal to the Society were fighting to save Isaiah, while those who had hated him were eager to see justice done. And some, it seemed, were just going crazy—settling old scores and letting the madness of the mob sweep over them.

Something crashed into the fort wall, shattering.

"We have to go," I said, pulling Becky's good arm over my shoulders and lifting her to her feet. She didn't fight it this time. I helped her put her oversize coat back on.

When we stepped onto the boardwalk, I froze.

The only light in the courtyard came from a dying camp-fire, sputtering red and yellow across frozen ground. A dark figure lay on the earth, next to the well. His leg moved, so I knew he was alive. A dozen people stood around him, laughing and jeering.

Someone stepped forward and kicked. Isaiah's back slammed into the stones of the well and he screamed.

I looked up and down the boardwalk, searching for help, but no one was there—just closed doors. Everyone was hiding or, worse yet, pretending to not know what was going on.

Another guy—someone tall and heavyset—jumped and landed with both feet on Isaiah's chest, and three more started kicking.

I'd seen this before, on the streets of Pittsburgh, when one gang found a lone enemy late at night in the wrong place.

"Benson." The word sounded almost like a gasp, like a cry. She wasn't trying to get me to help him now—there was nothing we could do, and we both knew it.

I had to get us out of there.

I stepped out onto the boardwalk and slid along the wall, trying to stay in the shadows as I inched us closer and closer to the gate. It would be guarded—it always was—but we had to leave.

"This is for Cookie." We were halfway across the courtyard from them, but I could hear the crack. I wasn't watching—my eyes were on the boards below me, trying not to make a sound—but Becky must have been.

"They killed him," she whispered. "They killed him."

I didn't look up. The boards were old and broken, and a misstep would mean noise and attention. I crept farther, remembering everything I'd been taught back at the school playing paintball—my heel touching first and then rolling my foot forward slowly, walking sideways and crossing my legs instead of walking forward. It was harder for Becky—she wasn't steady on her feet, and I was trying to keep her from falling.

The front door was getting close. I didn't know where we could go—Becky probably couldn't run, and I didn't know of anywhere else to hide than the Basement. We could go to the barn for now, or maybe get help from the Greens or some of the V's who'd just shown up. It wasn't much, but it was our best shot.

At least we had our coats.

"Hey!"

I didn't stop to look. I hurried to the door.

"They're coming," Becky whispered.

I ran, stumbling across the uneven boards.

The voices were louder, close behind us. "Where do you think you're going?"

I turned the corner to see Mouse at the door, a small lantern hanging on the wall beside her. A box cutter was in her hand, the blackened blade extended.

"Let us go," I said, but before she could answer we were surrounded.

"You were Society, too," said the guy in the front. I didn't know him, though I'd seen him in the fort before. Isaiah must have sent him to detention before I'd gotten to the school.

"Leave her alone," I said.

"Like she left us alone?" A chain was hanging from his hands.

"I didn't do security," Becky said with a wheeze. She was standing on her own, but bent slightly at the waist, and cradling her bad arm with her good one.

"You had the contract," another said. "You joined the Society even though you knew what they were doing."

Walnut took a step toward us. His hammer was wet with blood.

My legs felt weak. I hoped they couldn't see my hands shaking.

"Leave her alone," I said again. There was no threat in my voice anymore—I couldn't fight them, not all of them, not unarmed.

Someone pushed through the group, and as he moved into the light I could see his face. Skiver.

"You're with these guys?" I asked. "You're a jackass,

Skiver, but you're not a murderer."

He smiled. "You've been asking for it for a long time, Fisher."

Without waiting, he threw a punch. I couldn't move—I had Becky next to me and Mouse behind me—and the best I could do was try to deflect it. His fist skittered up my arm and into my shoulder, and I punched back. I hit his chest, but weakly.

Becky shouted something, and the rest of the guys poured over us. I fought as hands and arms tried to wrap around me, tried to hold me down. I elbowed a guy in the neck, and kicked another in the knee—hard—but it was like fighting a tidal wave.

Bright lights exploded in my head as someone hit me, and something got me in the stomach—I don't know whether it was a fist or a foot, but it felt like a freight train and I doubled over, falling to my knees. I waited for the next blow—the hammer, or the chain, or whatever else. But it didn't come.

"Pick him up," someone shouted, and an arm instantly snaked around my neck, pulling me to my feet and blocking my air.

The group was standing back a little, a small circle formed in the tiny alcove in front of the gate. Becky was on the ground, struggling to sit up. Skiver stood over her.

"Hi, Becky," he said, a low giggle escaping his lips. The

laugh rippled back across the group.

I fought against whoever was holding me, kicking backward, my feet searching for his knees, but I was losing air.

Skiver bent down, closer to her. "Re-bec-ca."

I reached back, uselessly trying to grab my captor's face, trying to gouge his eyes. I couldn't.

"Always so innocent," Skiver said. "Always telling everyone else what to do."

Becky pushed her back to the wall and gingerly stood.

Calmly, Skiver reached to her arm and squeezed her wound. She shrieked and slid back down the wall.

"Stop," I tried to say, but I couldn't force out the air. I felt my body growing weak.

Skiver touched Becky's face, and with an anguished scream she brought her knee up into his crotch. The mob howled in cruel amusement as Skiver reeled back. But it was only a moment, and he was on top of her, grabbing her by the neck and shrieking that she'd regret it.

And suddenly he was silent.

Mouse had stepped from the shadow by the door, her box cutter under his chin.

"You're done," she said. "Get back."

Skiver was motionless, his body frozen as his eyes darted from Becky's face up to Mouse's.

Mouse's words were quiet, but sharp and clear. "You get off her, or I gut you like a fish."

Slowly, carefully, he crawled backward. Mouse kept the razor tight against his skin until he was out of reach of Becky.

Becky's eyes were locked on mine, her face flushed and tearstained as she scrambled along the base of the wall toward the gate.

"You're done," Mouse said again, fearlessly staring down a dozen guys with only the small box cutter. She stepped back to the gate and pulled a rope. The warning bell clanged once, then twice. She pointed at me. "Let him down."

There was a pause, and then the arm around my neck released and I collapsed to the ground, sucking at the air. My lungs burned, and as I tried to move over to Becky I almost blacked out and had to stop.

She rang the bell again. "Birdman! Get out here!"

I heard the heavy clunk of the door being unlocked, the squeal of rusty metal as Mouse pushed it halfway open.

"What the hell is going on here?" It was Birdman's voice, somewhere behind all the guys.

We didn't stay. Regaining my composure, I helped Becky to her feet.

She touched Mouse's arm as we stepped out the door. "Thank you."

Mouse just shook her head without meeting our eyes, and then motioned for us to leave.

The fights outside were over. A few groups mingled together, picking one another up and wandering back to the Greens. As we walked away, three Society guys made a dash for the gate, likely to get inside and save their leader. I ignored them.

"Are you okay?" I asked her, crossing the road and walking slowly out into the field.

Becky nodded. "You?"

"I'm fine," I said. I stopped and pulled her scarf up over her mouth and nose. She stared back at me, her eyes showing more pain than she'd ever admit to.

I covered my face, too, and then steered us toward the stream. In a moment we were walking beside it, in the black shadows of the tangled trees.

"You're going to get better," I said.

"Of course," she said, and it sounded like she meant it. She was good at lying.

I looked back at the fort, now maybe a football field away. The gate was hanging open. I didn't know whether people had gone in or come out. No one was there.

Except . . . there was a kid standing on the roof, half-lit by the single small lantern. There was no way he could see us—it was too far, and it was too dark.

I thought it was Mason. I couldn't tell.

"Where are we going?" Becky asked. She was moving so

slow it could hardly be called walking.

"The forest," I said. "They can't get us out there. The implant won't let them."

"They can't, but Iceman can," she said.

I stopped at the stream and picked her up. I finally felt like I had the strength to not pass out and drop her, and keeping her dry seemed like the least I could do.

Her heavy coat was deceptive—she didn't weigh much at all, maybe even less than when we got to the town.

"Let's go to Shelly," Becky said.

"Skiver—all those guys—they'll find us."

"What choice do we have?"

I kept walking, past the commissary and the washroom, past the barracks, and stopped at the work site. "Can you walk?"

She smiled. "I'm not an invalid."

I set her down, and she did her best to hide the wince as she slipped out of my arms. I stepped into the construction site and tore a heavy sheet of plastic off a pallet of siding.

"Where are we going?"

"You grew up on a ranch," I said, directing her down toward the end of the road. "I'm going to ask you to tolerate a stinky night."

She shook her head. "Don't they check the barn? It seems too obvious."

I stopped and pointed at the tiny red structure beside the road. "I've never seen anyone check the chicken coops."

Becky stared for a moment, then laughed and leaned into me. "If I get bird flu, I'm blaming you."

Chapter Fourteen

The coop wasn't much smaller than the Basement. The birds were sleeping and hardly made a sound as I laid the heavy plastic on the floor and helped Becky down. I folded the plastic back over her like a taco, and then lay next to her, my arms around her to keep her warm. I listened to her breathing as she fell asleep.

The night was silent, and I strained at that silence, terrified of hearing a sound. A deer or a raccoon or another robot could stumble upon us while we slept, and there would be nothing I could do. We knew the chickens and cows were real—Birdman checked the cows the same way he checked the rest of us, and the chickens laid real eggs, and Jane said they'd occasionally cook one.

There wasn't much I could do if someone found us anyway. I had no weapons. Becky still carried Ms. Vaughn's Taser in the pocket of her coat, but it had already been fired and couldn't help us anymore. The hatchet I'd used on Iceman was back up in the Basement.

On the other hand, maybe Maxfield knew exactly where

we were, and how sick Becky was, and they didn't care. None of the dupes were active anymore, so it wasn't like there was a high demand for teenagers with implants in their heads. Maybe they were waiting for us to kill ourselves here in the town before they started anything new.

I was cold. My face stung. Frostbite was a real possibility, and I didn't know what to do to stop it. I fiddled with the hood of Becky's coat, pressing it down over her face as much as I could. It would have to do.

When the sun finally started to come up, I bent over Becky and checked her face, and I was relieved to see there was no frostbite. Her nose, mouth, and chin looked sunburned— the skin rough and splotched with red—and her lips were chapped and cracked, but it could have been a lot worse.

I felt some of the sting of frost burn on my face, but I had been better off than Becky. I was able to nestle my face into the back of her hood while she slept.

There was a tiny tap on the plywood door of the coop.

"Hey, Fish."

I froze.

"Fish," the voice said again. "It's me. Mason."

Slowly I peeked out the door. Mason was crouched beside the coop. He was alone.

"Hey," I said, not moving.

"Cold night?"

"We're okay."

I didn't like that he knew where we were, even if this was all perfectly innocent. If Mason had seen us, who else had?

"Got a minute?" he asked.

He was standing by himself, his coat off, and wearing only a flannel shirt, the sleeves rolled up. He looked tired.

"What's up?" I asked as I stepped out of the coop and scanned the tree line.

"I know what they did last night," he said. "It's not right, man."

I thought for a moment. "Which of the not-right things do you mean? There were a lot."

"I mean about the fight," he said. He paused, looking past me, and then off toward the horizon and the rising sun. "Is she okay?"

"Great."

"I'm sorry, Fish."

I stared back at him, but didn't say anything.

"It's not right," he said again.

Becky stirred, moving in her sleep and softly moaning at the pain in her arm. I closed the door and motioned for him to keep his voice down.

Mason was older than his dupe had looked. A little stockier, and he needed a shave. So did I.

"I don't know what happened," he said, still staring at

the coop like he could see Becky through the wood. "At the fence."

I shook my head. "We don't need to talk about it." I wasn't trying to spare his feelings—I just didn't want to think about it. I didn't want to hate him, but I did.

"I need to know," Mason said, finally looking at me. "What did I do?"

"Nothing," I said. "You didn't do anything."

"What did my dupe do?"

I ran my hands over my face and looked up at the brightening sky.

"You hit her," I said. "That's it. You chased us, and you hit her, and she fell."

"Hitting someone doesn't make them that sick."

"What do you care?" I said, suddenly angry. I took another step toward him. "What's it to you? You popped. The dupe wasn't taking orders from you."

"I care because it's important," he said. "I know what she . . . what she means to you."

I raised an eyebrow. *I* didn't even know what she meant to me. "Really? And what is that?"

Mason exhaled, frustrated. "What's your problem?"

"My problem? Someone got murdered last night, and then they tried to . . . Well, we're prisoners here, and Becky's sick, and you want to stand around and talk about feelings. You know what she means to me? She told me that she trusted me. No one trusts me—no one should, as you can see by all the people who got killed at the fence, and the next day, and last night, and probably tomorrow."

He started to speak, but I cut him off.

"Becky trusted me to get everyone out of the school, and now look at her. I need to make good on that trust. *That's* what she means to me. And I don't need you to come around here trying to apologize or whatever it is you're doing."

"But it's my fault," he said. "If she hadn't gotten hurt, you would have escaped."

I shook my head and turned back to the coop. "Too late for that."

"No," he said. "It's not too late."

I wanted to crawl back under that plastic and put my arms around her and wish we were somewhere else.

"They'll come take Isaiah's body," he said, speaking with more urgency. "They always do when someone dies, because they want the implant back."

I was going to have to hide—going to have to find a better place for Becky to recover. But I could tell that wasn't what Mason was thinking about.

"So what?"

"I'm going to help you get out," he said.

"Really."

"Yes, really. Last night those guys left the body out in

the road, but I moved it. It's in the stream."

I glanced over at the ford, but we were too far away to see anything. "Why?"

He spoke nervously, but with a glimmer of enthusiasm. Whatever he'd done, he was proud. "It's a trap. I got the idea about it the day you got here and Harvard hauled you into the forest. This is the first time we've had the bait to make it work."

"What did you do?"

"The body's in the stream, under some brush that overhangs the water. Iceman's going to have to climb in, jostle those branches. I ran some cables from the washroom lights, frayed them. I worked on it all night. He fights through the branches, the cable falls into the water, he's toast."

"Toast?"

"He's a robot, right? I bet he can still be electrocuted. Pop some circuits."

I paused and then gave a tired smile. "That's how we got you. Your dupe, I mean. Becky hit you with a Taser."

Mason looked uncomfortable, but laughed. "Then it works."

"What good does it do to fry him, though?" I asked. "There are more guards than him."

"He comes in the truck," Mason said. "He gets zapped; you take the truck and burn rubber to the highway."

I paused. It wasn't a bad plan. I peered off where the dirt road disappeared down into the stream. "Do we know where that road goes?"

"It has to connect somewhere," he said. "It's not like they built the truck here. Listen, it's getting light and he could come anytime."

"Becky can't go," I said. "She couldn't get to the truck fast enough."

"I'll take care of her here," Mason said. "We'll put her back in the Basement."

I felt panic boiling up inside of me. "I don't trust Bird-man. Not anymore."

"Then Shelly."

"I have to take care of her," I insisted.

"I'll do it," he said. "Now come on. I've got to get away from here so I'm not disabled right next to her."

He started walking backward down the road to the stream.

This was too much, too soon. I wasn't ready. I couldn't go without Becky.

"Do they have any other trucks?"

"What?"

"Do they have any other trucks?" I repeated. "How long will it take for backup to get here?"

He nodded. "I've seen three. There's the flatbed they

brought the lumber on, and two pickups, one white and one red. And we know there're at least four four-wheelers."

"So I could be driving back straight toward them, and they'll have two trucks. They could chase me, or block the road."

Mason shrugged. "You'll have to be better than them."

I looked at the road again. I'd bounced through foster care with poor families all my life; aside from driver's ed, I could probably count the number of times I'd driven a car on one hand. I'd never driven a truck.

"Do you know if it's a stick?"

He shook his head. "Don't tell me you can't drive."

"I can drive a little."

"You have to do this."

We were halfway down the road, and I turned to look at the coop. Maybe I could hide there with her and get her to the truck. But how would I know when Iceman got zapped? And the bigger problem: what if he parked on the wrong side of the stream? I'd have to pass him, through the stream, to get to the truck.

Maybe I could bring Becky with me now, across the field, and we could hide in the fort and wait.

The warning bell rang, breaking the early morning silence of the town.

We were running out of time.

I turned back to Mason, but he was nowhere to be seen. He couldn't have made it all the way back to the fort, and he couldn't be in the trees.

No, he was on the ground, face-first in the dirt.

Dread seized my whole body, pain running through my chest like a heart attack. I turned and ran.

They were coming. I could hear the truck now, its old unmaintained engine rattling through the trees.

Becky's head was sticking out the low coop door, watching me in confusion. She waved her arms frantically, urging me to go faster.

I stumbled with almost every step, tripping on the uneven ground, the knots of grass. I felt like the adrenaline and panic coursing through my veins were making me drunk, like I didn't know how to run anymore.

And then I was inside, and Becky and I dropped to the floor, collapsing onto the plastic.

I scrambled to look at the road, the coop entrance only open a crack.

I couldn't see anything, but I could hear the engine. It sounded like it had stopped on the other side of the stream.

Becky pushed the door open.

"Wait," I said, grabbing her coat.

"What?"

"Mason set a trap," I said.

She started to get up. "I know. I was listening."

"Where are you going?"

"To the truck," she said, her words punctuated with a wheeze.

"We don't know if the trap worked."

"There's only one way to find out."

"But what if it didn't?"

She looked horrible—her face burned by cold, her skin pale and sickly, dark circles under her eyes.

"We have to go now," she said. "Before someone else comes."

I stammered, trying to find a way to say no. I just wanted to stay here, for her to get better—completely healthy—before risking anyone's life again.

"You can't run."

"I'm not as bad as you think. And you can help me."

I looked back at the empty trees. Was the trap going to work? Would we just meet him face-to-face at the stream?

"Bense," she said, "we have to go."

"But . . ." We were going to die. *She* was going to die.

"We don't have time."

"I can't drive a stick."

Becky's cracked lips turned up in a grin. "Is that all? Do I have to do everything?"

She took my hand and coaxed me up, walking unsteadily.

"You do?"

She squeezed my hand. "I told you. I grew up on a ranch.

I've been driving old trucks since I was eleven."

I took a deep breath, and then pulled her good arm over my shoulders. We couldn't run, but we strode out onto the road, brazenly into the open.

CHAPTER FIFTEEN

I was moving as fast as I could, but it didn't feel like enough. It was taking too long, and the seconds were ticking away. We weren't going to make it.

I hedged my bets, leaving the road and heading for a thicker cluster of brush south of the ford.

"Where are you going?"

"He'll be heading for the ford," I said. "That's where the trap is set. I want to cross the stream somewhere else in case it doesn't work."

Becky nodded and pulled her arm away from me. "I can walk by myself. It'll be faster."

"I can carry you faster."

She took a breath to say something, but didn't.

There was still no sign of anything. I'd expected to hear a big electric crackle, or a pop, or anything. Maybe the trap didn't work—the wires didn't fall in the water. Or maybe they did, and he was built to resist electric shock. Or there was too much water and the electricity dispersed and didn't incapacitate him.

"Go without me," she said.

"No." We were almost at the stream.

"You don't have to protect—"

"Yes, I do," I said sharply. If she'd heard me talking to Mason about his plan, she'd heard me talking about her.

Her fingers dug into my shoulder. "Down!"

I was falling to my knees before she'd even said it. Iceman was on the road.

He wasn't looking at us—he was glaring down the road toward the barracks. He was dripping wet, and pissed off.

Becky was trying to pull herself with one hand toward the cover of the stream. With Iceman facing the other way, I risked it and jumped to a crouch. I grabbed the shoulder of her coat and pulled her into the bushes.

Without talking, we crawled farther, sliding down the stream bank to hide. We were still fifty yards of twisting river from the ford—from where Isaiah's body was. This felt safe. Relatively.

"Come to the fort!" Iceman bellowed, his voice unnaturally loud.

I darted across the stream, splashing through the icy water that was deeper here, and peered through the bushes at the fort. He was back on the fort side now, walking past his white pickup. We were too late. He was still closer to the truck than I was, and he had to be faster than me anyway.

Becky caught up with me just as a crack broke through

the morning silence like a gunshot.

Iceman had punched through the old wood of the fort's heavy door like it was glass. He reached between the shattered boards and unlatched it.

"This isn't good," Becky breathed.

"We need to get out of here," I said.

She looked back upstream, toward the truck.

"We don't have time," I said.

"I know," she snapped.

Becky stood, hunched over in what was probably just as much pain as it was stealth.

"Here," I said, reaching for her arm. "Let me carry you."

"I'm fine." She stepped from the bank into the stream, the frigid water rushing over her shoes and up to her calves. She paused to steady herself, and I reached for her again.

"Stop it," Becky said, her voice firm. "I'm fine."

I turned back to look at the fort. The gate was hanging open, and I heard the sound of something else breaking.

Becky was moving downstream, heading for the forest in short, unsteady steps. Our clothes weren't camouflage, but they were dark and we were still in the early morning shadows. Iceman had other things on his mind, too, but I had no idea how that would affect a robot. Could he get distracted?

The water was numbing my feet, but there was no other way to get back to the forest without climbing the bank and leaving the cover of the brush.

Becky moved slowly, constantly stopping to keep from slipping. She could only stretch out one arm for balance, and I heard her heavy breathing. The fast recovery she'd seemed to be making after Jane's help had reversed in the last twelve hours.

"Come to the fort!"

We both jumped, and she grabbed my shirt so she wouldn't fall. I looked back, but couldn't see anything—there was too much brush in the way.

"Come to the fort right now," the metallic voice bellowed again, sounding almost like a bullhorn, but deeper and louder. "Or I will fry your brains one by one."

Becky stepped back to the bank and knelt in a stand of scrubby willows.

"They're not looking for us," I whispered, dropping to my knees and crawling up the frozen muddy bank. He had to be talking about their implants.

She tried to stand, using the thin willow branches as support, but one snapped. We both fell, lying as flat against the earth as we could.

I couldn't see anything—not the field, or the fort, or Becky, or anything. The only sound was the burbling of the stream behind me. But I didn't dare move. My heart was pounding, thumping in my chest like a bass drum.

"Gather in front," the voice ordered, its deep, inhumanly loud sound seeming to rumble around the trees and town for several seconds before dissipating.

I rolled onto my side, and I could see Becky again. She was farther down the bank, kneeling and hunched over. She was cradling her bad arm with her good one, but the look on her face was one of determination, not pain.

I mouthed the words *keep going* to her, and motioned for her to head for the forest. She nodded, but it didn't look like she agreed with me.

Two cottonwoods grew ten feet upstream, their trunks almost touching at the bases. I slid back down the bank and crawled toward them. Crouching, I could see through the two-inch gap between them, my body still hidden almost completely.

Everyone—there had to be almost eighty with the new kids—was standing in the field. They were in groups, huddled together for warmth. Almost no one wore a coat, and one guy didn't even have a shirt. They'd been asleep when Iceman had come.

Mason was there, in the back. He looked like he was trying to stay out of sight, but Iceman must have suspected him. He'd been the only student outdoors.

Iceman stood by the gate, his back to the wall of the fort. I couldn't tell whether he'd been hurt by the trap. His clothes dripped and stuck to his body, but there were no obvious burn marks or mechanical problems. He looked as cold and evil as ever. And he was angry.

"We have exactly two rules for you," he said. He wasn't shouting, but his voice must have carried for half a mile. It was like he was talking into a microphone. "First, you're supposed to stay out of trouble. We haven't felt like it was important to elaborate on this order, because in the past you've all done a pretty decent job of this. It's been almost three months since one of your suicidal escape attempts, and it seemed like you'd managed to keep the peace."

I heard Becky moving toward me. I wasn't surprised that she'd ignored me and come back.

"We're constantly impressed by the new ways you idiots find of killing each other," Iceman continued. He was hardly moving—no hand gestures or even big facial expressions.

"Can I see?" Becky whispered, and I moved to let her peek through the trees.

"It's this new batch," he continued. "All you who tried to escape at the school. We worried that bringing too many at once was going to be a problem—you were too riled up after that disaster at the school. But I had sincerely hoped that your time in surgery would have let you cool down."

Becky slid back against the tree.

"He's not going to hurt them," she said, though it sounded like she was trying to convince herself. She wasn't looking at me, but staring straight ahead.

I peered through the trees again.

"You're kids, and you don't care about these things,"

Iceman said. "But what we've just done was not easy. Thirty-three students who needed implants. A dozen more who needed lifesaving surgeries. We have limited resources."

Someone shouted, "Screw you!"

Iceman stopped, scanning the crowd. "Who said that?"

No one made a sound.

He took a step toward them. "It would be better for you if someone answers my question."

The crowd started to stir, a few murmurs and hushed words.

Iceman folded his arms. "Fine."

The field erupted in screams as every student clutched his head and fell to the ground.

"We have to do something," Becky said, her voice quavering. There was nothing controlled or brave or tough about the noise—no one was gritting her teeth and fighting the pain—it was pure, anguished shrieking.

The screams stopped as abruptly as they began, replaced with soft moans and sobs as the tortured people lay on the cold earth.

"When you're ready to continue," Iceman said, "please stand. I can wait."

Becky looked at me. "Do you hear that?"

"What?"

"An engine."

I turned back to the road. The students were slowly

climbing to their feet, their faces red and tearstained. Some didn't look like they were even going to bother.

"Get up," Iceman said calmly. "I believe I've made it more than clear what happens when you disobey me."

The other truck appeared—a red one, speckled with rust and mud—and stopped in front of the fort.

One by one everyone stood, many standing together, holding one another up. Those who were alone looked unsteady, swaying drunkenly as they tried to regain composure.

Iceman walked to the truck and talked to the driver for a moment. Then he strolled back to the group. "As I was saying, this is all difficult. We're on a tight schedule, and frankly we don't have time to come out here and stop you disgusting larvae from killing each other."

The truck door opened and Ms. Vaughn stepped out. Her voice had the same amplified quality that Iceman's did. A chill ran down my body as I heard her speak—the last time I had, my knife was at her throat and she was laughing at me.

I wondered whether this was the same Ms. Vaughn, or another android version of her.

"Now," Iceman said, wiping his hands on his pants, "where were we? I believe I was talking about rules, and the first one was that you guys are not to cause trouble. That dead student there? That's what I would call trouble. The attack on one of your guards two nights ago? Trouble."

He scanned the crowd, waiting for a reaction, but no one stirred.

"We did surgery on that boy, and that takes time and resources, and you have all wasted that."

Ms. Vaughn spoke. "Malcolm King, please come here."

I didn't know who that was, but the only person who moved was Birdman. He strode to the front with as much bravado as he could muster.

Iceman still spoke to the group, not to Birdman. "We've given you only two rules because we thought it was best. The lack of restrictions increased your morale, and it required less oversight. However, it seems we will need to micromanage a little further."

He turned to Birdman. "You appear to be the de facto leader of this camp."

Birdman nodded.

Iceman faced the group again. "There are going to be changes. We don't like your meetings and we don't like your gangs and we don't like your secrets. From now on, there are no clubs or cabals or gangs or cliques or factions. You now have a third rule, and that's it: no more secrets. If we have to tear down every building in this complex and put you all in one big warehouse, we'll do it."

Birdman nodded again, a little more nervously.

Ms. Vaughn laughed. "Kid, what are you agreeing to?

You were in charge when everything went to hell."

Birdman dropped out of sight, but the gasps and screams made it obvious. They weren't torturing him. Birdman was dead.

Chapter Sixteen

There was a shout, and the crowd split, like the parting of the Red Sea. Suddenly Mason was running from the back, screaming as he charged Iceman and Ms. Vaughn with a long kitchen knife.

They watched him come, not even turning to fully face him.

Mason fell ten feet in front of them. It was like he'd been shut off. He skidded on the hard mud, face-first and limp and dead.

"Oh . . ." Becky said, but couldn't get out any more than that. They'd killed him, but it was worse than that. It was suicide. He knew what would happen—he had to know. He'd screamed, which warned them. He'd charged from the back of the group, not trying to sneak forward. He'd wanted to die.

Blood trickled out of his ear, dribbling in a dark thin line into the mud.

Becky turned and scooted back down the bank. I watched as Iceman and Ms. Vaughn cleaned up the mess, each slinging a dead teen over a shoulder as casually as if they were putting on a backpack to go to school. The two bodies were tossed into the back of Ms. Vaughn's truck. Someone yelped and sobbed.

Ms. Vaughn drove away, leaving the field full of horrified students to stare at Iceman.

Iceman walked back to his truck and pulled a sledge-hammer from the bed. All eyes were glued to him as he walked back to the fort's gate and smashed the hinges off the wall. With every swing he shattered the wood, pulver-ized the adobe, and mangled the steel. The gate was broken, but more than broken—it couldn't be hung again. The fort wouldn't be safe anymore.

Not like it was safe before.

Without a word, Iceman dumped the sledgehammer back in the truck, hopped in, and drove off toward the bar-racks. I had no doubt he'd be doing the same thing to those dorms.

I turned to look at Becky. She was crouched next to the stream, her knees to her chest as her good hand dangled in the icy water.

"I think we're safe," I said.

She nodded, not looking up.

"I don't think he knows we're here."

She nodded again.

Somewhere in the distance I heard the sharp crack of

breaking wood. Smashing the doors was just symbolic for Iceman, but it was going to be awful for the people who had to live in those barracks.

"You cold?" I asked.

Becky sat back, tucking her hand into her coat pocket. She stared at the water for a moment and then looked at me. She was good at putting on an optimistic face, but there was no pretense here. Her eyes were hard and hurt.

"You should have run."

I shook my head and looked away. "I couldn't."

"You should have left me in the coop."

"No."

She could be as brave as she wanted, but I knew the truth. She was cold and sick and unprotected. If I'd failed, she'd have been on her own. If I'd succeeded in stealing the truck they'd know that I'd been in the town and they'd come back looking for Becky. I just couldn't risk it either way.

The truck engine restarted in the distance. Iceman was leaving.

"Bense," she said. "I heard what you said to Mason. I can take care of myself."

I laughed, quiet and humorless, and looked at her. "Do you even remember what happened last night?"

"Bense . . ."

"Do you?" I said, raising my voice a little more. "You've got an infection, and you're trying to heal, and now you've got Skiver and whoever else to worry about."

"I'm glad you're helping me," she said. "I really am. But you have to quit babying me. If we don't get out of here then everything that's happened is a waste."

"Do you think I don't know that?"

I stood up and walked back to the trees. No one was in the field anymore, and Iceman was nowhere to be seen.

"When we were at the fence," Becky said, "and we ran, we knew we had to leave people there. They told us to run. They knew it, too—that it was the only way to escape."

I turned back to her. She looked so small below me, down at the bottom of the bank, crouched in a ball to stay warm.

"So what do you want me to do?" I tried to temper my voice, tried to sound calm, but days of frustration couldn't be held back. "The truck's gone. Mason's dead. I did the best I could."

She looked back at the stream, and then struggled to her feet. Her coat and pants were black with dirt.

"I'm not going to just head into the forest," I said. "Not until you're better."

Becky looked up at me, the hardness in her face replaced with something else—I wasn't sure what. She stepped into the stream, shuddering with cold as the water filled her shoes.

"Becky."

She just shook her head and kept her eyes on her feet.

She waded across and then climbed up the opposite bank. I hurried after her as she pushed through the willows, slowly and cautiously, wary of every difficult step. The long, thin branches whipped back at me as I followed her.

"Becky," I said again, and she turned.

"Don't think that I don't appreciate what you're doing—what you did," she said, fighting the tears in her eyes. "I do. You saved my life, and you've taken care of me every minute."

She paused, and I wanted to say something, but I could tell there was more to come. And I could tell I wasn't going to like it.

"I told you I trusted you," Becky said, now looking away so I couldn't see how fast the tears were coming. "But you don't owe me anything. If you had run for the truck, you wouldn't have been abandoning me—you'd be helping me. You have bigger things to do. You're strong and healthy and you need to get us out of here."

I exhaled, long and drawn-out, giving me time to think. Time to calm down and not just snap back. "I meant what I told him," I said. "I'm not leaving without you."

She spun back to face me. "Well, you know what?"

We stared at each other for several seconds as she fought for words.

"What?"

Becky took a breath.

"There are more people here than me. And I don't want to be the reason you're not helping them."

She turned and stepped through the willows. I followed. The green barracks were visible now, and the back of the commissary. Some of the kids were on the road, but it didn't look like they'd seen us.

"Just . . ." she started. "Just . . . forget it."

"Becky."

She didn't stop, but she was still having trouble walking. I stepped in front of her.

"Look," I said, my voice beginning to shake, "I'm sorry I didn't run to the truck. But I couldn't leave you alone. You trusted me."

Becky pulled her hood off and brushed her unkempt hair from her face. "You're acting like this is some kind of debt. Like you owe me something."

I started to speak, and she stopped me.

"I'm going to see Carrie and Curtis," she said. "They're going to help me, and you'll be free to do whatever you need to do."

"That's not what I want."

She shook her feet—they had to be freezing—and then looked back at me. "Well, so what? You can help people— you're the only person right now who can—and you're not doing it. And I don't want it to be because of me."

I didn't know what to say.

"Let me help you get back," I said.

"I'll be fine."

"No—"

I tried to take her hand, but she pulled away and shot me a dark look.

"Benson, I didn't trust you because I liked you. I trusted you because you earned it. You never stopped fighting, and you were trying to help, trying to convince all of us."

I opened my mouth to say something, but she held up a hand to stop me.

"I'm holding you back," she said finally. "I don't need you to take care of me."

"But—"

She turned away from me, head down. "I don't know how else to say it, Bense. I don't want to say it." There was a long pause. "I just can't trust you anymore. Not when we're together, at least. You'll do better alone."

I watched her walk the rest of the way across the field. I didn't know what had happened. She hadn't understood, and I didn't know how to explain myself.

I didn't want her to have to take care of herself. I wanted to help her.

I sat down on a broken log and waited, making sure she made it to the dorm. There wasn't a door anymore, but a girl met her on the steps—I couldn't tell who it was—and took Becky by the arm.

What was I supposed to do now?

Was it time to escape? To pack supplies and brave the forest? Maybe it wasn't as scary as I'd thought—we'd spent the night outside. Maybe I could do it.

But I didn't want to do it without Becky.

I was freezing—my feet and legs were shaking. I didn't have any real desire to go back to the fort, but that was where my dry clothes were, so I headed over. As I got close, I expected to see something, some sign of what had just happened there—blood, maybe. But the only thing that looked out of place was the debris from the gate.

At first glance, nothing looked different inside, either. A few people were on the boardwalk, and someone had started a fire in the pit. But there was complete silence. Harvard was in the courtyard, standing alone, gazing motionless up at the sky. Mouse, still in her pajamas and bare feet, sat on a bench, her legs pulled up to her chest. She was rocking slightly, eyes closed. Walnut sat on the edge of the walkway, and he looked up when I passed. Neither of us said anything.

Lily's door was closed, and I knocked. The old wood rattled.

I had to do something. And maybe Lily could help. Lily wouldn't have waited for Becky—she would have run for the truck. She'd have gone for help.

There was no answer. I knocked again.

"She's not here."

I turned to see Jane. She wore the same thin coat and jeans as when I'd first seen her in the barn, and her short hair was matted from sleep. She walked up to me, looking closely at my face. "Are you okay?"

"Yeah."

She touched my forehead with one finger, gently tracing a line over my eye. "Does that hurt?"

"I didn't realize anything was there." I touched the spot and felt a tender bruise. "I hadn't noticed."

"You look cold," she said, and turned toward the fire pit, where a few others were gathered. She nodded for me to join her.

I followed. Harvard was still staring at the sky. I wondered if he was going to lose it. I had a hard time thinking anyone missed Birdman—but it's not like Harvard was the nicest guy, either. They were a good fit. Mouse, too.

Jane and I sat on the edge of the boardwalk, close enough to feel the heat. I stretched my legs out, edging my cold feet toward the fire.

"Mason liked you," Jane said. "A lot."

I nodded.

"He was lonely," she said. "I mean, his dupe was. But the real Mason felt it. You changed that."

"I hardly even talked to him since I got here." I glanced over at her. She'd been watching my face the whole time, studying me. She smiled a little, and then turned to the fire.

I took off my damp shoes and propped them on a rock to dry out. Steam rose off my socks as I held my feet up to the heat.

"Mason tried to escape this morning," I said.

Jane was plainly shocked.

"He tried to electrocute Iceman," I said. "That's why Isaiah's body was moved to the river."

Jane narrowed her eyes. "Why would he do that?"

"He was trying to help me—kill Iceman, then I take the truck and leave."

One of the other girls spoke. "You knew about this?"

I shrugged. "He told me maybe five minutes before Iceman showed up. I didn't have time to do anything." It was a lie. I knew Becky had been right. I could have done something.

"Iceman wasn't electrocuted," one of them said.

"No," I said. "It didn't work." I didn't even know whether that was true. It might have knocked him out for a minute, maybe more. He was soaking wet—maybe he'd fallen in.

"Did Mason ever tell you where he was from?" Jane asked.

"New York, I think." I pulled my socks off and laid them on one of the rocks surrounding the pit. My feet were white. I sat on the dirt, closer to the fire.

Jane climbed off the boardwalk and sat down beside me.

"He wasn't from New York," she said. "He just told people that. He was a runaway. He grew up on a farm. Arkansas, I think."

"Really?"

"He wanted to get out of here more than anybody," she said. "He actually has a family somewhere."

"I thought Maxfield didn't take kids with families."

Jane shook her head. "They take people no one will miss. He'd been on his own for a long time—maybe a year—when he ended up here. He was depressed. Before you became his roommate, we all were worried Maxfield would kill him, like Dylan."

I looked back at the fire. One girl stood and put another log in the center. The fire licked it, surrounding it with bright yellow flames until the edges turned black and the log was just another part of the blaze.

"They can't keep this up," I said.

The other girl spoke. "Look where you are. They were here a hundred years before we showed up. And they're going to be here a hundred years after we're gone."

Harvard, who was far enough away that he probably couldn't hear us, laughed.

The girl pointed at him. "You know what's happening to him?"

I watched him. He was still staring at the sky, a grin on his face.

"A nervous breakdown?"

She rubbed her hands over her face and stood. "Feed-back."

I looked at her, and then back at him. This wasn't like when Shelly was getting feedback. She had to sit down, looked like she was fighting a bad headache. Harvard was in a trance, or high.

"They started," Jane said. "A couple others, too, during the night."

"The school's using dupes again?"

Jane sighed. "That's what we're here for."

"I should have run," I said.

"What?"

"Mason told me his plan. I should have gone faster."

Jane didn't respond.

I stared into the fire. "I'm going to leave."

Her voice was small. "When?"

"As soon as I can pack." I pointed over at Harvard. "I need to talk to him, too." I still hadn't heard whether he'd discovered anything during the dissection.

"It's not safe out there," Jane said.

"Safer than staying here."

I was trying to convince myself that I was going because I had a duty to go. That this was still about Becky's trust, about the calls of the wounded at the fence as they urged me to run for help.

But the truth was, I wanted to leave now because everyone would be safer when I was gone.

"Birdman used to say that the point of the fort was for escape," Jane said, leaning forward and stretching her hands toward the fire. "He'd tell people that we had all the security here because we were planning something. But he wasn't. He never was."

"So why did he keep it so secure?"

"Paranoia," she said. "Whatever else Birdman was, however he acted, he was scared. I mean, he could get in fights and intimidate people, but he was terrified of Maxfield. He hated having them in his head."

"But . . ." I said, and then couldn't think of anything to say.

I watched as Harvard sat down, the otherworldly smile still gleaming on his face.

"Some people like it," Jane said, noticing where I was staring.

"Like the feedback? Why?"

"Depends on what's going on. Everyone likes it if it's good—you can't help it. But sometimes even the bad stuff is better than being here. It's like living another life."

I wondered what Harvard was seeing. Was he back at the school? Was Maxfield repopulating the school with dupes so they could bring in a fresh batch of humans for their tests?

I remembered my first day there—how excited I was as

I drove up. It was the nicest school I'd ever been to. Well maintained, everything worked, good food. Looking back, I realized the problems seemed easy. I wanted my freedom, and the gangs were hurting people, but no one was dying. There wasn't the constant suffering like there was here.

I looked back at Jane.

"You know what I liked about you?" she asked. Her voice was quieter, more guarded. She massaged one hand with the other, gazing at her fingers like they were suddenly very interesting.

"My amazing ability to get into trouble?"

Jane smiled. "I've been here a long time, and you've seen what it's like. It's tolerable, and sometimes it can even be fun, but most of the time it's just boring and depressing. I loved my dupe. I loved her life, and I looked forward to the feedback. And when you showed up, well . . . I had a lot of feedback while you were with me. It was like I was always at the school."

I stared at her. Her eyes were tired and her face bore all the marks of years of manual labor and exposure to the elements. But she was happy. No, it was more than happy. Content. It was an emotion that I didn't know if I'd ever felt, a state I'd never been in.

I kissed her.

Her lips were soft and warm, and she turned and leaned into me. I touched her face, my hands on her freckled cheeks and running through her hair.

She put her hands around my shoulders, pulling me closer.

I wrapped her in my arms, kissing her cheek and then holding her tight against me.

But when I opened my eyes, pulling back to kiss her again lightly, something was wrong. It wasn't with her. She grinned back, the happiest I'd ever seen her. The contentment from her eyes was now written all over her face.

But something was wrong with me. Because when I leaned back to look at her, I was almost startled. Like I didn't expect it to be Jane. Like I didn't want it to be her.

"If I remember right," Jane said, our faces only inches apart, "I should probably watch my back about now."

I smiled, though I could feel my stomach dropping. I looked behind her. "All clear."

"Good." She pulled me close and laid her head on my shoulder.

I let out a long, tired breath. "I have to say, I'm impressed. You're the first person I've ever met who can joke about how she was beaten to death."

She laughed and turned again to face the fire. I put my arm around her waist, pulling her against me as we watched the flames. But it still didn't feel right, and I knew exactly why.

"I need to ask you something," I said.

She took a breath. "I wish it could wait."

"I don't think it can."

She put her hand on mine. "Don't do this again."

"What?"

Her tone was serious now, the life and contentment gone. Even her hand felt cold. "When you kissed me before—when you kissed my dupe—it didn't end well." She laughed quietly. "And I'm not talking about being murdered."

"You tried to get me to stay," I said.

There was a long pause. After several seconds, she finally spoke. "I'm glad you didn't stay there. I'm glad you came here."

I nodded, trying to think of what to say next. I liked Jane. I liked her a lot. But she wasn't Becky.

"So ask me," Jane went on, a slight edge in her voice.

"I don't know what to ask," I finally said.

Lily appeared at the gate, walking into the courtyard carrying a shoe box. As she approached us, she raised her eyebrows and smiled. Then she reached into the box, pulled out something wrapped in cellophane, and tossed one to each of us.

"Cupcakes," she said, rolling her eyes. "Just came up in the commissary's elevators. I guess this is Maxfield saying, 'Sorry we killed your friends. Have a cupcake.'"

It wasn't a typical breakfast, but I tore mine open. The food in here was much more basic than what we'd had at the school, and I hadn't eaten anything sugary in days.

"Benson was looking for you," Jane said.

She laughed. "Looks like he found you first."

Jane blushed and focused on her cupcake.

Lily's eyes met mine, and I gave her a look indicating that we needed to talk somewhere else.

"They're divvying up the food," Lily said. "You ought to head over there before the good stuff runs out."

Jane took a bite of the chocolate cake. It was factory-made, mass-produced stuff, but as Jane ate it you'd think it had come from a five-star restaurant. She licked a stray bit of frosting from her lip and smiled at me.

"You want to go?"

"You go," I said, and leaned forward to check my wet socks. "I'm going to change clothes."

She took another bite of cupcake and stood. For a moment, a mask of seriousness crossed her face. She knew what I was thinking. She knew what I was going to do to her. Again.

"Don't go anywhere," she said, her voice artificially cheerful.

I nodded.

CHAPTER SEVENTEEN

So, you and Jane, huh?"

Lily plopped down on a bench in the meeting room and set the box of treats on the floor beside her. I stood at the window, watching people wander over toward the commissary.

No one had cleaned this room since the events of last night. Some benches were shoved to the wall, and others overturned. The sheets of fabric—all of Birdman's meticulous, paranoid notes—were scattered on the floor. No one cared anymore. I picked up one of them, looking at the detailed map of the underground complex. Notes marked the items in the room, the color of the paint, the places where guards usually stood.

I shrugged.

"Does Becky know?"

"If she doesn't already, she will soon."

"Did you bail on her, or did she bail on you?" Lily asked. She wasn't even looking at me—all of her packaged food was lined up in rows on the bench in front of her, orderly and categorized.

"Both?" I said, leaning back against the cold adobe wall. "I don't know. She bailed on me first, but I deserved it. I don't want to talk about it."

Lily selected a row of granola bars and began organizing them by flavor. She was either obsessive or bored.

"Then what did you want to talk about?"

"You told me that Birdman wasn't trying to escape, that Shelly was."

She nodded.

"I want in," I said.

"You heard the rules," Lily said with a sardonic laugh. "No more groups."

"I think if we're trying to escape, it's okay to break that rule."

She held the box to the edge of the bench and swept all her goodies into it. "First, I can't get you in Shelly's group, because I'm not even in it."

"Then how do you know it exists?"

"Just observation. Birdman grilled me about the underground complex, but Shelly grilled me about the forest—about where I'd gotten to and how I was caught."

I looked back out the window. From here, I couldn't quite see the ford.

A tall brown-haired girl was alone, sitting cross-legged in the road.

"Someone's getting feedback," I said.

Lily moved to the window. "Eliana. Interesting."

"I heard a lot of people are now," I said.

Eliana was far away, so it was hard to be sure, but I thought she was crying.

"They are," Lily said. "Maxfield's starting up the school again."

She turned away from the window and faced me, arms folded. "You'll have to talk to Shelly. She runs the show, and she doesn't tell anyone everything. But I don't know why you're dealing with this. Gather supplies. Get out of here."

"Isn't that what you tried?"

"And I made it pretty damn far," she said, annoyed. "I just didn't have any weapons. But you've got anything you want—hammers, knives, shovels."

"What if I go for help and they find out? What'll Maxfield do then?"

"They'll chase you."

"Or they'll kill everyone here and burn this place to the ground to hide the evidence."

Lily didn't have an answer to that.

I pulled up the hood of my sweatshirt and started for the door. "I'm going to find Shelly."

"At some point you need to just take care of yourself," she said.

"I'm not leaving without Becky."

Lily turned, a small smile on her face. "Don't you mean Jane?"

I stared back at her. I didn't know what I meant.

No. That wasn't true. I meant Becky. No, that wasn't true either.

"I'm going to get *all* of us out of here."

Maxfield couldn't win.

Chapter Eighteen

I walked out into the courtyard and sat down beside Harvard. He was still grinning, and I didn't even know whether he could talk.

I waved my hand in front of his face. "You there?"

He turned his head, but not far enough to look at me. "Benson. Hi." He talked slowly, like he was strung out on some drug.

I couldn't believe I was coming to him for help when he was like this. But I was out of options.

"Hey, Harvard. Snap out of it." I slapped his back. "I need to talk to you."

"They're at the school," he said dreamily. "The sisters. The ones we were talking about."

"I don't care," I said. "I need to know what you found out about the android I brought you. Anything useful?"

"Why would they be there?" he murmured. "They've seen the underground complex. They're talking about it."

"What?"

He wasn't really talking to me—he was staring at the sky,

but obviously seeing something I couldn't.

"I don't think they're dupes. I think they got the implant, and then went to the school. They're warning the other students."

That didn't make any sense.

"The android," I said. "Anything?"

He turned his head slightly. "The heart."

"What about it?"

"I love this," Harvard said. "I haven't been active for so long."

"What about the heart?"

His voice was euphoric. "It's an artificial heart. The whole thing was beautiful. It's not gears and gizmos in there. It's like a human, but fully artificial. It's . . . elegant." Harvard finally looked at me. "It's shoved over to the side. Because there's a power source in the direct center of the chest."

"So what?"

"I don't know," he said, drifting off again. "It's amazing. But that heart . . . it's not protected, and it actually juts out into the left armpit."

"The armpit?"

"He had a bump in his armpit," Harvard said. "Like a design defect. I bet we could use it to tell dupes from humans." He drifted away for a moment. "You should get an implant. This is wild. There are a lot of new students. More every hour."

I swore under my breath, and then looked around his room.

"So that's all you can tell me? A bump in the armpit?"

"It's more than a bump," he said, finally looking at me. "It's the miracle you're looking for."

"What do you mean?"

"The heart is unprotected there. Smack that bump and it'll push the heart into the power source. Should shut the whole robot down. I tell you, it was beautiful."

He turned back to look at the sky, and then closed his eyes and began to hum. That was all I was going to get from him.

Harvard's "miracle" was a little bump in the armpit. I was hoping for a whole lot more.

I met Jane on the boardwalk as she was coming back from the commissary. Her box of snacks was smaller than Lily's, with more granola bars and fewer sweets.

I made up an excuse about needing to take a shower, but the truth was that I couldn't bear to look at her. It wasn't that I didn't like her—Jane was fun and beautiful, and had this been some other reality I probably would have been following her around town like a drooling idiot.

But now it was different. And she knew it. She'd known it the minute she'd left the fort, and even though she smiled at me, I could see it in her eyes. She knew something was wrong, that I'd betrayed her again.

So I left Jane at the fort. I hoped she'd go back to her room and scream at the walls and tell her friends how much she hated me, how much of a jerk I was, how much she wished I'd just leave this stupid town for good.

I wanted her to say that, to think that. It'd be so much easier if she hated me.

I hated me.

I climbed back into the Basement and found another set of clothes. They weren't exactly clean—nothing here was very clean—but they were dry, and they'd been up against the wall that the Basement shared with a fireplace, so the shirt and jeans were warm. I wanted to pull them on right then, but I forced myself to head to the washroom.

There was no wait at the showers, and for a moment I thought I was really lucky. But the lack of wait was due to a lack of hot water. I still showered, mud and grime speckling the floor of the stall and swirling down the drain. Everything about this place was filthy. Now that Birdman's power was gone, and the false security of the fort's door had been beaten to dust, would everyone move into the cleaner, nicer barracks?

As I watched the dirt swirl around the drain, I wondered where the pipes went. Was that mud and grime all washing down to some enormous septic tank? Or did the pipes flow away from town and dump into a river somewhere? I guessed it was the septic tank. Nothing ever got out of here.

I dried off and got dressed, and made a halfhearted effort at washing my other set of clothes, my old Steelers sweatshirt and torn, muddy jeans, and then left the washroom to hang them on the clothesline—inside out, so the logo wouldn't show. My clean coat had a hood, and I still had my scarf to obscure my face. I was glad I got here during the winter—it made hiding so much easier.

The commissary crowds had dissipated when I went inside. I knew most of the few people left in there, but no one wanted to talk to me. Maybe they blamed me for what happened to Birdman, or maybe they knew I'd kissed Jane, or maybe they just hated me. There were plenty of other reasons.

Six large cardboard boxes sat on one of the tables.

Almost all the treats were gone. A box of granola bars was empty of all the good flavors—the chocolate chip and peanut butter—leaving only about forty-five oatmeal-raisin ones. There weren't any candy bars or cupcakes or Twinkies. I took the last of the sweets—a banana-flavored MoonPie.

What was left was probably more useful for me, anyway. It didn't look like anyone had touched one of the boxes—it was still three-fourths full of beef jerky, Slim Jims, and, at the bottom, small packages of crackers.

I grabbed as much as I thought I could carry, making a pile on the table. If I was going to be escaping—whether it was hiking out to the road or following the trucks—I was going to need supplies.

There weren't any more little boxes like Lily and Jane had, so I walked to the back of the kitchen to find something to carry my food.

It didn't look like they did a lot of cooking here. There were two big ovens and a long grill, but I doubted it was feasible for feeding eighty people. Each day's food came up through the elevators, just like at the school.

I opened a cabinet and saw huge packs of plastic forks, napkins, and paper plates. Nothing was organized. No one had jobs here. The few real tasks that people did were voluntary, or ordered by Birdman. Jane milked the cows because she liked the animals. The guys who'd been working on the barracks were doing it because they didn't want to share with the newcomers. But it looked like no one ever volunteered to straighten the kitchen or sweep the floors.

I opened the elevator, just to look inside. It wasn't disguised like the closets back at the school. This was obviously something unusual—a metal door about four feet tall and three feet wide. Inside it was a dull gray, but clean, and I could feel a breeze coming from the quarter-inch gap at the threshold.

I stretched my foot inside it, giving a little shove on the floor to test its strength. The elevator bobbled slightly.

I had an idea.

* * *

The barrack was full, and the chatter quieted as I stepped through the broken doorway. No one seemed to be doing anything special—just twenty people massed around the small fireplace, blankets draped over them while they talked and played cards.

At the far end of the building, Becky sat with her back to me, talking to Curtis and Carrie and taking notes in her journal.

Someone touched my arm before I'd made it five steps in. Shelly.

"What do you want?"

"I need to talk to Becky," I said.

"She's busy."

"I'll wait."

Shelly folded her arms. "I'll send someone to get you when she's ready to talk."

"This is important."

"And you're a jackass."

"I know."

Shelly pulled me to the corner of the room. Her voice was hushed.

"She heard about Jane."

"I was going to talk to her about that, too."

"It's a little late."

"That's not why I'm here."

Shelly took an annoyed breath, looking over at Becky.

"Listen," I said. "I know that you're taking care of her because I was being a jerk—I was. But you don't have to protect her from me."

Shelly was obviously ready to unleash a tirade. I stopped her, holding up my hands and taking a step back.

"I'm terrible. I know. But I need *you* to know that there's no one on this earth that I care about more than her."

"Tell that to Jane."

"I think she already knows," I said. "But I'm not here to talk to Becky about that—I'm not here to apologize or beg her to take me back or anything."

Shelly raised an eyebrow. "You're not here to apologize?"

I smiled. "There will be a lot of apologizing, I'm sure. But I'm here to talk about something else."

Shelly looked back at the crowd around the fire. It was too loud for anyone to hear us.

"You're leaving?" she asked.

"Maybe."

"You can't take her with you."

"I know."

"So you're just saying good-bye?"

I shook my head. "I need her help. She's smarter than me. I need your help, too, if you're willing."

Shelly sighed. "Okay. But she's in the middle of something. Let her finish."

"What's she doing?"

"Interviewing," Shelly said. "You know, like Birdman used to do. We do it, too. Curtis just got here, and we want to know what he saw."

I nodded, and sat on the floor to wait.

I had so much to tell Becky. Maybe she'd hate me because of Jane. I could understand that. But sitting here, watching her, I promised myself that I was going to do everything I could to make it right.

Shelly sat across from me.

"It's over, you know," she said.

"What is?"

"Our escape attempts."

"So you were trying?"

"I was. But that ended long before you got here."

"Why?"

Shelly sighed. "Nothing worked. We've got these things in our heads, and we can't cross the perimeter. We tried everything. We made a helmet, worked on it for months, trying to get the densest metal we could find—"

I chuckled. "Like Magneto."

"Exactly," she said. "But it didn't do a thing. It still hurt when we went into the forest, and they could still track us—a four-wheeler was out patrolling ten minutes after we crossed the border."

"What if it is like Harvard said?" I asked. "What if there's a transmitter out there, and if you get too close to it, then it hurts? Couldn't you just get past the transmitter—deal with the pain—and then it would hurt less the farther you went?"

"Tried that, too," she said tiredly. "But you can't just deal with the pain. You go too far into the woods and you pass out." She crossed her arms and stood up. "Trust me. If you can think of something, we've done it. You know why the Basement is called the Basement? Because we have an underground bunker—a real basement that we dug, trying to tunnel out of here."

I sat back, stunned. "Seriously?"

"So we named the thing in the fort the Basement to throw them off."

"Why didn't Birdman hide us in the real basement?"

"Probably because he wanted to keep an eye on you."

"So the tunnel didn't work?"

She shrugged. "It's deep. I seriously doubt they can track us down there. But we got a few hundred yards and ran out of materials."

"Materials?"

"For supporting the roof so it doesn't cave in. We steal stuff when we can—we skimmed some of the lumber from the new barracks and told them they didn't send enough—but we have no idea how far we have to go. A mile? Fifty? And we kept running into bedrock. Heck, we even ran into the cement ceiling of the underground complex."

"So it's just a big cave."

She was annoyed. "Yeah. Not much good."

"So you have nothing else? No secret plans? Ever thought of starting a forest fire to get attention?"

"Tried and failed." Shelly shook her head. "We're out of ideas, unless you know how to build a radio or something."

"Then I'm going to go," I said. "But I need help."

She looked at Becky. "And you've come to get it from her? A lot of nerve."

I nodded. "I know."

Someone was shaking me. I must have fallen asleep.

It was dark. The fire was out, but moonlight streamed through the drafty windows.

"Bense."

It took a moment for my eyes to focus, but I knew the voice. Becky was across from me, sitting up, touching my arm.

Someone was next to her. Carrie. And Curtis. Shelly was on my bed, by my feet. Lily leaned against the wall.

I looked back at Becky. "What's going on?"

Shelly was the one who spoke. "We're here to help."

I didn't take my eyes off Becky. It was hard to get her facial expression in this light. She knew about Jane. She had to hate me, and I expected to see it on her face. It had to be there—it was just too dark.

"Is it safe to talk?" I whispered.

Shelly answered again, pointing to the room behind us. "I trust everyone here. And most people are asleep. That doesn't mean it's safe, but it's the best we can do."

I turned to Lily. "I thought you weren't involved."

Shelly smiled. "If there's anyone who pesters me more than you, it's Lily. She's in."

"So you're really leaving?" Becky asked.

"Yeah," I said.

"When?"

I wished it was just the two of us talking. I had things I needed to say. They would have to wait.

"A couple days," I said. "I've got some things to do first."

Curtis leaned forward, his elbows on his knees. "That's what we're here for. We want to help."

"Tell us what you need us to do," Shelly said. "We could create a distraction or something. And I've been stockpiling supplies."

I took a breath. It was time to stop being scared.

"Not the forest," I said. "I don't even know which direction to run to get to civilization, and they've got too many cameras to hide from."

"How else are you planning to get out of here?" Shelly asked, exasperated. "A hot-air balloon?"

"No," I said. "I've only got one chance. What are the odds

205

I actually make it out of the forest alive? And if I do, what are the odds I will have made it out of there undetected? And if Maxfield knows I'm gone, then what are the odds that they'll just sit here and wait for the SWAT teams to move in?

"Maxfield would evacuate you," I continued. "Or kill you, so my escape wouldn't mean anything."

"Maxfield might just escape and leave us here." Carrie's voice was full of nervous hope.

"Or they might burn the whole place to the ground," Lily said.

"If I escape, then I'm getting the rest of you out of here." I met Becky's eyes. "Everyone."

Curtis scoffed. "How? You're going to do surgery and take these things out of our heads?"

"Nope," I said. "I'm going to turn them off."

No one said anything.

"Birdman has been keeping records of every little thing that happens in the underground complex," I said.

Becky finally spoke. "No. You can't."

"I'm not going into the forest, because I can't save the rest of you that way. I'm going down the elevator in the commissary. They won't see it coming. I've gone over the maps and I've read the notes. They don't have a lot of guards down there, because—"

"Dude," Curtis said, cutting me off. "We've been there.

You can't just walk around."

"You've been there when they're ready for you," I said. "They wait for you at the bottom of the detention elevator, and they take you to a cell, and you never go anywhere unescorted. And you're not armed."

Carrie's voice was almost pleading. "But you've seen what they can do. They're too strong."

"I've killed dupes," I said, trying to sound confident. "I killed Joel's dupe with a pair of garden shears. Becky got Mason with a Taser. I took that guard out a couple days ago with Shelly's hatchet."

"But could you fight more than one at the same time?" Curtis asked.

"How many have we ever seen at once?" I asked. "The other day there were three guards on four-wheelers."

"There could be a hundred," Shelly said.

"No one has ever seen more than two Icemans and one Ms. Vaughn at one time."

"That's optimistic," Shelly said sarcastically.

Curtis shook his head, his voice rising slightly over our hushed tones. "That's not optimism. That's stupidity."

"No," Becky said, her eyes fixed on mine. "I think he's right."

Now it was my turn to be surprised.

"I think it's genius." She turned to the others. "You guys have an implant in your heads so you can't cross into the forest, right? Well, that implant didn't hurt you when you were down in the complex, did it? You can't go out, but you can go in."

I hadn't thought about that, and my heart jumped; I was suddenly anxious. I didn't want to lead another revolt.

But she was right.

Shelly was smiling now, too, and Curtis. Only Carrie looked scared, and she gripped Curtis's hand. She'd just gotten Curtis back and now he could die.

I looked at Becky and sighed. "I come to you with a plan to sneak in alone and you suggest a war."

She just grinned.

Chapter Nineteen

We agreed to meet in the morning, somewhere more private, to make the real plans. I wanted to stay and talk to Becky alone, but we were all together and there wasn't a chance. We looked at each other for a few seconds before she turned and went back to her bed. I lay down in front of the fire and thought about the mess I'd created until I fell asleep.

I got up just before dawn and left the barrack. There were things I needed to do before the town woke up.

When I reached the stream, much of the water was crusted over with ice. That seemed to come and go almost every day.

I stepped across. I'd gotten used to it now, knowing exactly where to step to move quickly and stay dry. I hadn't thought I'd be here long enough to learn those kinds of things about this town.

The fort was quiet. There was no fire in the pit, or even lingering smoke or embers. One of the rooms on the far side of the courtyard had a small sliver of light escaping through a crack in the door. Other than that, the entire place was still.

I didn't walk on the boardwalk. It was too loud. I crept along the dirt and weeds of the courtyard, choosing each step with care and pausing at every slight sound. Finally, I had to step up onto the boards—one, two, three quick steps—and I was at the door of the meeting room.

It hung half-open. I stepped inside, peering through the darkness. No one was there.

It didn't take me long to gather up every scrap of the cloth maps. Some were still rolled, and others were tossed carelessly on the floor. I spread out the largest and laid the others on top. There were around twenty or twenty-five, and when I finally rolled them all up together it was as thick as a bedroll. I slung the heavy cloth over my shoulder and stepped back outside.

There was a little more light, but not much. The fort was still quiet, a mass of shadows.

Three steps across the creaky boards and I was back down on the ground. I darted across the courtyard to Carrie's room. In less than a minute I was in and out, the maps over one shoulder.

I hadn't gone two feet when I heard another footstep on the boards. It was close.

I didn't turn to look. I ran.

"Benson," a voice called in a loud whisper.

Jane.

I turned back. In the darkness her silhouette made it look like she was wearing a dress, but as she got closer I could see it was her apron. She was heading out to milk the cows.

"What are you doing?" she asked as she reached me.

"Getting blankets," I lied. Whether she believed me or not, I had no idea.

"Come on," she whispered, and started toward the gate.

I should have stopped her right there, but I was too worried about the noise. I didn't want to talk in the fort.

We walked down the road. Frost crunched under my feet, and every breath let out a cloud of silvery ice. Even the cloth maps were cold.

I didn't know what to tell her. I could say that I shouldn't have kissed her, that it was a moment of weakness, that I didn't even realize what I was doing. But that wasn't true. It didn't take a moment of weakness to kiss Jane—it took a moment of daring.

I could tell her that it was because she and I couldn't agree. Because we had no future. Because even if I had Jane and we could be together here, it wouldn't be enough for me. I needed freedom.

But that was a lie, too, or only part of the truth. Yes, I wanted freedom, and I could never be what Jane wanted—I could never enjoy staying here, not for a year or a month or a week. But that wasn't it.

It was because I loved someone else more. That didn't even sound right—that made it sound like I gave Jane three stars and Becky four. It wasn't like that. It was that, despite everything wonderful about Jane—everything I loved about Jane—I was still *in* love with Becky.

I was in love with Becky.

"I'm leaving," I said.

Jane stopped. We were standing at the stream, its water murmuring beside us as it fought its way through the ice and rocks.

She faced me.

"Yesterday . . ." I stammered. "I shouldn't have . . . I—"

Her whispered words were so quiet I could barely hear them. "I know. I knew yesterday."

I stared back at her, wishing I could see her face, her eyes, and not just the dim blur in front of me.

"I didn't mean to hurt you," I said, knowing immediately how stupid it sounded.

Her head moved. I couldn't even be sure whether she shook it or nodded.

"I'll be here," she said weakly. "When you come back for us."

I wanted her to scream. I wanted her to call me a liar and a player and a bastard. I wanted her to slap me.

"Good luck," she said. Her hand reached up to my face, and her lips touched my cheek. "Please be safe."

Jane pulled back her hand, paused, and then hopped quickly across the stream, darting from rock to rock in the darkness.

We met in the barn, after Jane had finished with the cows and left. Gabby was with us now, too, which made seven. Of that seven, three were wounded. It wasn't exactly the best revolutionary army.

We sat just inside the open door, with Gabby perched on the threshold to watch for trouble. I'd laid the largest, most detailed map out on the floor in front of us, and we gathered around it on our knees.

"It looks accurate," Shelly said, "from what I remember. It's been a long time."

"It looks good to me, too," Curtis agreed. "This is where the detention elevator goes down, and this is that first hall." He traced his finger along a corridor. "They took us to this waiting area, and from there I went to a surgery room." He studied the map for a moment, closing his eyes to think, and then tapped the map again. "I think it's this."

Gabby shook her head. "I wasn't conscious for any of that. I woke up in the cell."

"They're like hospital rooms," Curtis said, searching the map for them. "Except they have bars like a prison. It's where you recover after surgery."

I'd seen rooms like that on the map. "These?"

He and Gabby both inspected them. "I think so. Yeah."

Shelly held up another piece of cloth. "I think this is a more detailed map of that."

The floor plan on that map was darker, with a lot more written in the margins. It looked like any and all details people remembered had been included—one note said the walls were white tile, and another said one of the bars on a certain cell was loose.

Becky tapped one of the scribblings and read it aloud. "'Pass code for cell number nine starts three-seven-eight.'"

"How do the pass codes work?" I asked, looking at Curtis and Gabby. "The note says you can reach the keypad from inside the cell?"

Gabby shrugged. "Think of a jail cell, but it has a keypad instead of a keyhole."

"You're in there for a long time," I said. "Can't you just mess with it and figure it out?"

"No," Carrie spoke up. "If you put in the wrong code an alarm goes off."

"The only problem with this map," Becky said, "is that it doesn't have any information about where that commissary elevator goes."

"None of us ever got that far," Curtis said, and tapped the cell map again. "All we saw was surgery, the cells, and we walked through this other section when we were leaving."

Shelly sat back. "That brings up the big question. What's our goal down there?"

I dug through the other maps and found one that was significantly different. While the others were quickly sketched and covered with scribbles, this one was finely drawn, annotated with clear lettering and even illustrated. It was drawn on the back of a torn white T-shirt, and labeled CONTROL ROOM.

"I read through it this morning," I said. "Birdman was the only person to ever go there. It says he escaped at some point and opened a lot of doors trying to find his way out. He got captured here. This map was his personal drawing."

I laid it out for the rest of them to see. The room was long and narrow, lined with things that Birdman had marked as "machines" and "monitors." At the far end were two chairs in front of a row of computers, and something on the wall that looked like a window that curved inward. From the care he took with this map, it was obvious Birdman knew it was important.

We all stared at it, reading the notes. They were very descriptive—talking about the colors of the lights, the size of the monitors, the polished cement floor—but nothing that explained what we were supposed to do when we got there.

It was Shelly who finally spoke. "If we go in there and start flipping switches, we could kill someone."

"We'll have to figure it out. It's our only chance."

We stared at the map. Everything that kept us captive here might be destroyed in that room. Could we turn off the implants? Turn off Iceman and Ms. Vaughn? Maybe even call for help?

"I'm going," I said. "You guys don't have to."

Shelly shook her head. "Of course we're going."

We spent the rest of the day memorizing the maps. Carrie got some charcoal from the fire, and we took turns trying to redraw the floor plans from memory, right there on the barn wall. While one person sketched, the others would watch and correct. After several hours, all of us could remember the hallways and label the main rooms, and even some of the smaller ones.

"What about weapons?" Gabby asked as dinnertime approached.

Shelly leaned back against a wall and tiredly ran her hands through her hair. "We have a small stockpile. Knives, spikes, some homemade brass knuckles. And, of course, all the tools from the work site and the barn. A lot of nasty stuff we haven't had a chance to use, since they can just stop us with the implants."

Carrie looked at me. "They're going to do that, you know. As soon as we get down there."

"I've thought about that," I said. "I'm going to be the

distraction. I go first and they start coming after me. You come down after. Since it's only me, they might not shut you guys off so fast."

"And me," Becky said.

We all looked up at her. She was doing so much better, but I knew how quickly things could take a turn for the worse.

But she insisted she could do it. It was time for me to start trusting her.

"You and me," I said.

Lily spoke, changing the subject. "When are we going?"

"Not tonight or tomorrow. We need more time." I did my best not to look at Becky. We didn't need more prep time; I wanted her to recover as much as she could to give her a fighting chance.

"Oh," Curtis said, a broad grin breaking across his face. He sat on a cot and took off one shoe. "I wore these old crappy shoes for two years at the school. They're falling apart."

He pulled out a torn piece of the insole and set it down beside him. He looked at Carrie and winked. "You always—" He stopped, and then looked back at the shoe, his voice quieter now. "The other Carrie always told me to spend some points on a new pair, but now I'm glad I never did."

The insole out of the way, he fished inside and then reached out his hand to me.

"Been giving me blisters for a week," he said, dropping

two bullets into my hand. "Thought they'd come in handy."

"But we don't have a gun," Becky said.

"We can make a zip gun," I said.

Everyone just stared at me.

"Don't you guys watch movies? A zip gun. It's basically a homemade gun—you put it together with a little pipe for the barrel, and some other stuff."

Curtis looked skeptical. "Do you know how to do it?"

"Not really. I was kind of hoping one of you did."

Shelly took the bullets from me. "Lucky you've got a Louisiana girl here. We can make a powerhead."

"What's that?"

"You kill gators with 'em," she said with a smile. "It's like a spear with a bullet on the end. You jam the end of the spear into something, and the pressure pushes the firing pin on the back of the bullet. Kills the alligator."

I laughed. "That's perfect." I looked around at the group. "Anyone else have any hidden weapons?"

Becky reached into her coat pocket and pulled out the Taser. "I've been carrying this around, but it's already been fired."

Without a word, Gabby took it from her and pulled off the cartridge at the front, then flipped a tiny switch and pulled the trigger. The front of the Taser popped and buzzed.

Becky's mouth dropped open. "You mean that thing's worked the whole time?"

Gabby smiled and handed it to me. "It only fires darts once, but it still works if you touch someone with it."

Carrie laughed. "I think I'm the only person here who doesn't know freaky things."

That night we slept in the barn. The others in the camp might have suspected something was going on, if they were paying enough attention to care. But everything was in so much disarray now that we weren't too worried.

I'd heard Skiver moved into the fort, and a lot of the other Havoc guys I'd hated. Things were quiet now, because of what had happened to Birdman, but it wouldn't be long before the power vacuum was just too appealing and the thugs began to flex their muscles. Someone was going to start taking control again.

If this attack down the elevator worked, it wouldn't matter.

Shelly and Curtis sat by the lantern during the night, fiddling with the powerheads. They'd gotten metal pipes from the washroom—breaking two of the sinks to do it—which they were using as barrels, and after trying half a dozen different handles, they settled on long screwdrivers. These wouldn't be spears, but I was still thrilled to have them—fourteen-inch-long sticks that fired a bullet when you rammed them into someone. I hoped I'd get to use one on Iceman.

Carrie sat beside Curtis, watching him work. They seemed happy together. Awkward, but trying to figure it out.

Gabby read the maps over and over, backward and forward. When it got dark, she closed her eyes, her hands gesturing left and right. She must have been visualizing walking down the corridors of the complex.

Lily watched the doors, anxiously moving from one to the other, fiddling with gear, wandering around the barn.

"Do we know how to get into the elevator?" Becky asked, lying on her side on a pile of old hay.

I sat near her feet. We'd been together all day, friendly and uncomfortable and not discussing anything.

"It's just housed in cinder-block walls," I said. "We can break the walls and then rappel down. We have rope."

"That'll be loud."

"We'll have to be fast."

I wanted to say more to her, but I couldn't think of anything that didn't sound awful.

"I need to ask you something," she said quietly.

My stomach lurched.

She turned and looked at me, right at my eyes. Her face was lit orange by the lantern, her brown hair glowing like copper.

"But first," she said, "I swear I'm not trying to make things weird. I'm not. This will sound a little backhanded, like one of those things girls do to tear each other down. But

I swear that's not what I'm doing."

"Okay," I said. "Go ahead." I should have said more, but I could hardly speak those single syllables.

"Jane patched me up when I first got here."

"Yeah," I said. "But don't think anything about—"

"That's not what I want to talk about," Becky said quickly, holding up her hand to stop me. "No. That's . . . that's different."

"Okay."

"I took a shower yesterday," she said. She touched her arm. "It's crazy. Maybe I don't remember right, because I was so sick and it was always so dark in the Basement, but my arm was torn up pretty bad, right?"

"It was horrible."

She sat up, pushing her thin blanket off. She wore a plain white T-shirt, the sleeve cut off at the shoulder. Her arm wasn't in the sling now—she'd removed it to sleep—but it was wrapped in new gauze.

She stretched her arm forward, like she was reaching toward me, and then up to the ceiling, and then out to the side.

"It doesn't make sense," Becky said. "It's like it's just regrowing. There's even skin on it—new skin, not scabs or anything."

"I know. I saw it starting to regrow when we were in the Basement. I don't know how it's happening."

Becky motioned for me to sit by her, and she slowly began unwrapping the gauze. The skin underneath was red and puffy and smooth, but had grown entirely back over the wound.

"Does it hurt?"

"Not much. It's really tight."

"That's incredible," I repeated.

She stretched her arm out again. "Mind helping me rewrap it?"

"Sure."

Becky straightened her arm, resting her hand on my shoulder. I carefully adjusted the bandage and began wrapping.

"So," she said, looking at my hands, not my face, "the reason I'm asking about Jane . . . She couldn't have done this. Even a real doctor in a hospital couldn't have done this—not this quickly."

I kept rolling the bandage.

"Jane had a packet of powder," I said. "It looked like Kool-Aid. And there was some tinfoil-looking thing."

"I saw that when I took a shower. I threw it away."

I nodded, trying to think of something to say. "The robots can heal really fast."

Her eyes went wide, and then her face contorted in revulsion.

"No!" I said, laughing. "I'm saying I think Maxfield has

that kind of technology. The robots bleed, and their skin feels and looks like ours. They have to know a lot about anatomy and medicine. Jane was just using what was in the first-aid kit."

I pointed over to Gabby, now asleep on her cot. "She should have been dead. And Curtis—people thought he was going to lose his leg. The school can heal humans. We're valuable here. Well, the kids with the implants are valuable. The school is going to make sure they stay alive, and they have crazy advanced medicine to do just that."

I finished wrapping the bandage and tried to tuck the end under to secure it. She flinched.

"Anyway," Becky said, "I'm sorry for implying that Jane was . . ."

She lifted her arm off of mine, flexing her biceps and testing the bandage. I grabbed her hand and held it.

"Becky," I said, my heart racing. "I know what people told you about me and Jane."

Her face flushed. "You don't have to—"

"Just listen," I said. "What they told you was true. I kissed her. And I've regretted it ever since."

"Stop. You don't have to explain."

"I want to."

She looked up at me, her eyes finally locking on mine. "When I came down from the Basement, when I first talked to Carrie . . ." Her voice trailed off, but her gaze didn't.

She took a deep breath. "I asked Carrie about David," she blurted out, and then her voice quavered. "You never knew him. We used to be together. A long time before you ever came to Maxfield. I thought . . . I thought, maybe . . ." She looked away, at Carrie sleeping on the floor beside Curtis, her fingers touching his leg while he worked.

I nodded. Mason had told me that Becky had a boyfriend who was killed in the war. I hadn't even thought about it, but as soon as she found out about the dupes, she must have wondered whether there was a human version somewhere here.

In a way, this town gave some people a second chance. But not everyone.

"I don't want you to go down the elevator," I said.

She squeezed my hand. "I'm going. My arm is a lot better."

"I know."

"I'm getting stronger every day."

"I don't want you to die."

She wrapped her arms around my neck and nestled her head in my shoulder. "We'll make it out of here," she said. "You and me, together."

CHAPTER TWENTY

Curtis and Shelly finished the powerheads several hours later. There was no way to test them—we only had the two bullets—so all we could do was hope.

We watched for the last lanterns to be extinguished in the other barracks, and then we waited for what felt like at least two hours after that before leaving the barn.

Gabby and Carrie were asleep, and the five of us didn't wake them as we carried the weapons outside.

"There," Shelly said, pointing to one of the chicken coops—the one Becky and I had stayed in.

"Seriously?" I asked.

Shelly grinned. "I hide things well."

It stank, and there was chicken crap and loose feathers all over our plastic blanket now. Once all five of us had crammed inside, Shelly shooed some sleeping birds out of the way and pulled up a loose piece of plywood on the floor.

It was the tunnel.

There was a sturdy ladder made of rough-cut two-by-fours, and we slowly made our way down. It was deeper than

I expected, the dirt sandy and coarse. At the bottom—a full twenty feet underground—there was a small room, large enough for the five of us to fit comfortably. The tunnel, maybe three feet by three feet, extended off into the darkness.

Everything she'd mentioned was there, though some of the metal weapons had rusted. She said they had been stored here for at least nine months, and water from the fields must have seeped in. Still, there was plenty to use. She'd stockpiled it in anticipation of a more widespread revolt; there was more than enough for the seven of us.

We added the two powerheads and the Taser to the supplies. We couldn't risk losing them now.

"Tomorrow night, after dinner," Shelly whispered as I closed the box. "We'll create a distraction and try to get as many of the androids here in town as we can, and then we'll follow you."

"What are you going to do?" Becky asked, shivering a little.

"I don't know," Shelly said, a look of mischievous glee on her face. "Maybe we'll burn something down."

Lily grinned. "I volunteer for that."

Shelly kicked away the dirt under her feet. She held the lantern out and pointed toward the smooth, flat surface she'd just uncovered. "This is the roof of the underground complex."

I knelt down and felt the solid, thick cement. The gravity of what we were going to be doing sank in.

I looked up at Shelly. "Any chance we could tunnel through here? It might be less noticeable than breaking the elevator."

Curtis answered. "It'd take days, probably, and I doubt it would be any quieter. We'd need the pick. And who knows how thick that cement is."

I nodded.

We all stared at one another for a few moments. This was real.

We were going inside tomorrow. Soon this nightmare would be over.

It was well past dawn when I woke. The girls were still sleeping, but Curtis sat at the door, staring out at the fields. Snow had started to fall, but it wasn't sticking to anything yet.

"Coast clear?" I asked, standing behind him.

He shrugged. "You think this will work?"

"Tonight? I hope so. If not, I'll be joining you in the implant club."

"I had that feedback stuff all night," he said.

"Really?"

He looked up at me. "It's like a dream, but you know it's real."

"Where's your dupe?"

"Back at school. Like nothing ever happened. The first minute I was aware of him he was in the car, going through the gate again. Ms. Vaughn was driving."

"So they're just dropping him off like he's one of the human kids?"

He nodded. "There were others in the car. Humans. Kidnapped. They're scared." He looked over at me. "They never used to do that before—kidnap people. Everyone who arrived at Maxfield wanted to be there."

I patted him on the shoulder. "We're going to stop them."

"Yeah." He didn't sound convinced.

I pushed past him and out the door, hopping down to the ground. "I'm headed up to the fort. I want that hatchet."

"'Kay."

There was a little activity in the barracks as I passed— talking and laughing from one, small plumes of chimney smoke from two more.

I could see a bunch of people getting feedback. Anna, one of the old V's, was sitting on the ground in shorts and a T-shirt, a bath towel in the dirt beside her. She looked like she'd fallen over, but she was smiling. Something good was happening somewhere.

I picked up her towel and draped it over her goose-bumped legs.

There were three more incapacitated, all in the road. One was close to the river, and her friend was sitting next to her, making sure she didn't fall in.

Things were happening in the fort. Six guys were already up and in the courtyard. It looked like the fresh lumber from the work site had been brought up here, and they were fixing the boardwalk.

Mouse sat on a bench, watching them and sipping something steaming from a metal cup. She scowled when she saw me.

"Is that a new coat?" I asked her as I passed by. Instead of the old too-big leather jacket she always had on, she now wore a long double-breasted wool coat that hung almost to her knees. It looked far too stylish and clean for this town.

"Maybe if you'd go outside once in a while you'd get a new one, too," she said. "New shipment came yesterday. You missed it. What are you doing in that barn, anyway?"

"Nonstop party," I said. I noticed now that four of the six guys had new coats, too.

"Where are you going?" Mouse called as I kept going.

I didn't answer. It wasn't like she couldn't see across the courtyard.

I knocked on Carrie's door, just in case someone new had moved in. There was no answer. I pushed it open.

The place had been ransacked—all her boxes were overturned and empty, and the blankets and mattress had been taken from the bed. Most of the pictures from her walls had been torn and trampled on the dirty floor. The cloth mural was gone, but the wooden panel remained in place. I pulled it out and climbed up into the Basement one last time.

The hatchet was just where I'd left it, the android's blood still staining the wooden handle.

I dropped back down into Carrie's room. I took a final look, and then stepped outside onto the walkway.

One of the guys was on the ground. They all were, a long two-by-four lying across one of their chests.

I ran into the center of the courtyard. Was it feedback?

Mouse was slumped over on the bench, her steaming coffee now spilled and seeping into the boards beneath her.

"No."

There was a rumble somewhere, like the truck but louder.

Iceman was coming. And Becky was alone on the far side of town, asleep.

Dammit. There hadn't been a warning bell. With Bird-man gone, were there even guards on the roof anymore? I ran to the broken fort door. A truck was coming into view. I could go hide in the Basement, but that wasn't going to save Becky.

I ran for the ladder that led up onto the roof.

Whatever was rumbling was big—bigger than the pickup I'd seen. Was it the flatbed? Bringing more lumber for the work site?

The awning was a mess of loose shingles and decaying

wood. I scrambled up and onto the adobe roof, dropping flat to hide.

What *was* that noise?

My heart was pounding like a bass drum, even louder than the increasing roar of whatever was coming down the road. I scooted across the roof, trying to find the balance between silence and speed. When I peeked over the edge, I had a view of the stream and the tops of the barracks. I didn't see anyone—human or android.

There wasn't time to wait or to think. I slid over the edge, the weather-beaten adobe crumbling to dust under me, and dropped down to the ground outside the fort.

Pain shot through my legs, and I sprawled forward onto my face, getting a mouthful of cold sand. The hatchet flew from my hand, tumbling across the frozen grass.

I left it. Waking Becky was more important. I fought against the pain and climbed to my feet, racing across the frozen ground toward the cover of the stream. It wasn't far—maybe fifty yards—but it was out in the open. All I could hope was that Iceman had gone into the fort.

Adrenaline coursed through my veins, and I didn't feel anything as I crashed through the dry branches of the trees and splashed down into the stream. It wasn't until I was on the other side that I dared turn and look behind me.

There was no sign of what was making the huge noise.

I could see the front of the parked truck, but not Iceman.

The snow was falling a little heavier, but not enough to block my view.

I crept up the bank, my panic receding. I had to think, to move quieter and smarter.

I ran from building to building, crouching low and judging my footsteps carefully. After the noise I'd made in the trees, the fear of stepping on a twig was probably unfounded, but I avoided them anyway. I stopped at the cement wall of the washroom and listened, then ran behind the first barrack and did the same. It probably took less than two minutes to get from the stream to the barn, but it felt like an hour.

Curtis had fallen from the doorway and lay on his side in the dirt, a small scrape on his forehead from the landing.

I jumped past him and into the dark, silent interior.

The four girls all still lay on their cots, motionless.

I ran to Becky's side, shaking her awake.

She opened her eyes slowly. "Bense?"

"Iceman's here. We have to get to the tunnel," I said. "Now."

I ran back to the doorway.

"Dammit."

"What?" She was behind me now, peering out the door.

The red pickup was coming down the road. It had passed the washroom.

I ducked back inside. "They'll see us."

Becky didn't wait. She ran to the back of the building, darting around our collapsed friends, and to a window. I followed.

"What about them?" Becky said, motioning to the immobilized girls while she tried to shove the window open.

"They'll be fine," I said, adding my strength to hers. "Maxfield only wants us."

"Unless they know about our plans."

The window was stuck. Nothing in this barn was built right. The window frame was probably out of square.

I could hear the truck now.

Becky told me to move, and almost before I could she smashed a piece of firewood through the glass. The shattering sounded like an explosion.

She ran the wood along the edges of the broken panes, knocking out the small remaining shards.

The truck stopped right outside.

The last thing I saw as I fell from the window was Ms. Vaughn in the doorway, staring at me.

Chapter Twenty-one

S he's coming," I said, grabbing Becky's hand and running for the forest.

Ms. Vaughn shouted something behind us, though I couldn't make out a word. I hoped she was yelling at us, not calling for backup.

The ground was uneven, dense with tangled brush and fallen branches, and Becky and I were both struggling. We'd failed. They had come straight to the barn, so they must have known what we were doing, what we were planning. We'd been too careless, too public. We hadn't posted constant guards to make sure no one listened at the windows. We discussed too much in the barracks that first night.

Becky stumbled on something and grunted, and I turned again to see Ms. Vaughn. She was gaining on us.

Becky turned down a slope, running along the center of a dry streambed. But it was rockier than it looked, and steeper, and we had to go slow. I searched for a stick, something to even the odds, give me a fighting chance.

There. A broken limb of a pine tree, about as thick as a baseball bat and maybe three feet long. I could grab it as I ran, scoop it up and spin around and hit Ms. Vaughn. She'd never see it coming.

Becky stumbled on a loose patch of pebbles, and then I did, too. Neither of us fell, but Ms. Vaughn was right behind us. I was fifteen steps from the limb.

Becky turned, up and out of the dry streambed.

Dammit.

I followed her, leaving the limb. Ms. Vaughn's footsteps were loud and close.

No more time.

I turned at the top of the slope and jumped, screaming as I did it. Ms. Vaughn tried to stop, tried to raise her Taser, but I collided with her and the two of us tumbled back down into the stream.

I smacked at her armpit, like Harvard had told me, but now realized how useless that was. Unless her arms were above her head, it wouldn't ever be exposed.

I grappled with her, but she was far stronger than me. I pounded my fists down into her side, but her arm was in the way.

Becky was there, a branch in her hands.

Ms. Vaughn got her elbow around my neck, and then punched me in the back. Pain burst across my ribs. I gasped for air.

There was a crash, wooden and hollow, and Ms. Vaughn dropped me.

I sucked at the air, forcing myself to stand.

Ms. Vaughn was between us now, her scalp bloodied. The branch in Becky's hand was broken, only about a foot long. She changed her grip, threatening to stab with the sharp, jagged points.

"More are coming," Ms. Vaughn said. "Give up." She glanced back behind her.

As soon as she looked away, I jumped at her. Becky shrieked and—

Pain rocketed through my body, a sudden intense ache that was both sharp and dull, abrasive and blunt. I collapsed to the ground, unable to move.

I couldn't think. I was seeing things, but they were a fog. I couldn't force myself to understand them.

Becky. Ms. Vaughn.

I'd been Tased. The electric darts were in me somewhere, but I couldn't tell where. I couldn't move. I couldn't think.

Then Ms. Vaughn fell. Becky was next to me now, swinging her bloodied stick at something in the air.

I took a breath. The paralysis was gone, but the pain was still there.

"Bense," she said. The long electric filaments were

tangled around her stick, and she threw it aside.

I sat up, and my eyes went wide. I had time only to point. Ms. Vaughn was up again, and she pounced.

I was weak, unable to make my muscles move the way they should. Becky was on the ground, pinned beneath Ms. Vaughn, screaming.

I put one foot under me, and then another. I felt drunk.

Ms. Vaughn punched, and Becky yelped.

I grabbed Becky's stick, shaking off the Taser's wires. I tried to take aim, but was unsteady on my feet. I had no strength.

Ms. Vaughn had something silver—handcuffs. She slapped one onto Becky's wrist, and then roughly rolled her onto her face in the dirt, fighting for her other hand.

I brought down the stake, squarely into Ms. Vaughn's back.

The tip drove into the skin, but only an inch, and I couldn't do any more. In a flash, Ms. Vaughn whipped her arm out, hitting me below the knees with the strength of a bear. I dropped.

Ms. Vaughn had Becky's other arm now—her injured arm—and was cranking it behind Becky's back.

I lashed out again, and Ms. Vaughn batted me away in one fluid motion.

I landed face-first in the dirt, dazed, and as I turned my

head I saw it. The discarded Taser.

I tore off the cartridge, like Gabby had done, flipped a switch, and rammed the sparking gun into Ms. Vaughn's neck.

Without a sound, Ms. Vaughn collapsed, falling on top of Becky and then rolling down into the center of the stream. She was lifeless, limp and silent.

Becky was gritting her teeth, sitting up and cradling her injured arm against her chest.

I dug through Ms. Vaughn's pockets and found the truck keys, but the handcuff key wasn't there. I stuffed those into my pocket and kept looking.

"How did you stop her?" Becky said, standing. I handed her the Taser.

"I can't find the key."

"It's okay. We need to go."

I took her hand and we jogged ahead. We had no food, no weapons. Becky didn't have a coat. We couldn't escape now. We'd have to wait until things died down, and get back inside. Maybe our attack into the elevator could even still work.

I couldn't see the town, but I smelled the wood smoke. And even out here, I heard the rumble. It was still there.

"Thank you," Becky said after several minutes. "For coming for me."

"Always."

* * *

By the time we made it back, we could hear four-wheelers in the forest behind us. They were searching.

We crouched in a patch of tall grass at the tree line and watched the town. There was a cloud of dust in the center, swirling in the cold wind.

"Are they grading the road?" Becky asked.

"I don't even know what that means," I said with a smile.

Becky smirked. "We can't all grow up in the country. Only the lucky ones."

"It sounds like an engine. But something big."

Becky turned and looked back into the forest. "We need to get out of here."

I pointed to the fort. "If we can get back into the Basement, we can hide there until they leave."

"Which Basement? The fort or the tunnel?"

"The fort. We can't lead them to the tunnel."

"Back into the center of everything?" she said, and stood. "Well, at least they won't be expecting it." She was pretending to be healthy, but her breathing had been labored since the fight, never really calming back down, and her hand shook in mine.

We walked the perimeter of the town, staying deep enough inside the trees to avoid being seen. It took about ten minutes to get behind the fort. From the back we couldn't see any sign of the androids. Even the rumble seemed to have dissipated. I couldn't hear the four-wheelers anymore.

We waited and listened. Nothing changed, in front of us or behind. There wasn't much here—no reason for anyone to be watching. In all the time I'd been at the town, this was the first time I'd even seen the fort from the back.

"Run or crawl?" I asked.

Becky let out a quiet, wheezy laugh. "They both sound so great."

"I can carry you."

She shook her head. "I'm fine. I vote run."

We took off. It wasn't far, but it felt awful—exposed and dangerous. Becky was beside me the whole way, ignoring the pain in her arm as she ran at full speed. We both hit the adobe, falling into a crouch along the base of the wall.

I moved to the nearest window and peered in. The room was empty, but I could see through the door to the courtyard beyond. A few guys were standing and talking. A girl sat on the boardwalk, getting feedback.

"They're awake again," I whispered to Becky. "Iceman must have left."

We crept around the side of the fort, cautiously watching and listening. No one on the road, no one by the trees or down by the ford.

I gulped a deep breath and then took Becky by the hand. We stood, turned the corner of the fort, and ran for the front door.

Everyone looked at us as we entered, murmurs bouncing around the courtyard, but we didn't stop. Becky led the way to Carrie's room, throwing the door open. No one was inside.

I slid the bed over to the wall, and in a moment Becky was up in the Basement.

"I'm going to find the others," I said.

Becky frowned, looking down at me. "Can't you wait?"

"I'll be right back. It's okay. They're gone."

I hopped to the floor and pushed the bed away from the wall. Becky watched me from the hole.

"Hey," she said as I touched the doorknob.

"Yeah?"

She smiled. "Hurry back."

"Three minutes, tops."

Becky pulled the panel into place, and I rehung the torn mural hiding the Basement entrance. I stepped outside.

Everyone was staring at me.

I crossed the courtyard to where Mouse was sitting. Harvard was beside her on the bench, grinning and dazed.

"You're alive," she said. Her face was red, angry.

"What happened?"

She shook her head. I noticed she had a scrape on her cheek, probably from where she fell when the implant immobilized her.

"What was the dust?" I asked.

Mouse snorted in disgust. "You didn't see?"

"No. Just saw dust."

"They flattened the commissary. Bulldozed the whole thing, one big heap of rubble."

"What?" That was it. Our attack was over.

"They'll be trucking the food in now."

"Did they say why?"

Her eyes, which had been darting around the courtyard, focused on me. "No. But I imagine we have you to thank?"

I shook my head and turned to leave. Our plan was destroyed. I'd have to go out through the forest.

I headed for the barn. I needed to find Shelly and the others. Had Maxfield punished them for being involved?

"Where are you going?" Mouse called after me.

"Why do you care?"

The last thing I wanted was to stay in that fort and talk to Mouse and her cronies. I jogged down the road, ducking through the trees and crossing the stream. All the rocks were out of place, the ford now a mass of mud and debris where the bulldozer had plowed through. I had to step in the water, but I didn't care. I had other things on my mind.

The air was still laced with dust as I climbed the bank and saw what was left of the commissary.

They hadn't flattened it, like Mouse had said. It was just the back, where the elevator had been. They knew what we were planning, and they were sending a message.

There were people all around, some staring at the demolition, others sitting down getting feedback. The school had to be in full swing, and emotional—they were probably seeing all the new kids coming. There would be fights and crying and arguing. And the school was kidnapping now, too; at least when I showed up there was some pretense that Maxfield was a good thing.

I left the commissary, jogging through the crowd to the barn. No one was outside, and when I jumped up to the door I saw it was empty. Had they been taken?

I wasn't worried now. I was mad. The message Maxfield sent today wasn't to anyone else—it was to us, to me. They knew I was here. They could do whatever they wanted, and I couldn't stop them.

I ran up the steps of the nearest barrack and looked in.

"Anyone seen Shelly?"

Nothing but shaking heads.

I hopped down and ran to the next. I was about to ask again, but Gabby was right inside the door.

"You're okay!" she said, jumping up and hugging me. I could see Shelly over Gabby's shoulder, wrapping a bandage around someone's head.

"I'm okay."

"What about Becky?"

"She's fine—"

243

We all heard it at once. It was impossible to ignore. Engines. Lots of them.

I looked out the door just in time to see someone on a four-wheeler zipping in across the field. I heard others.

There was a thud behind me, and then another and another. Gabby fell, knocking against me before she smacked her head on the floor.

It was a trap.

They must have seen us come back. They knew we would, and they left spies.

I jumped down. The four-wheeler I'd seen wasn't heading toward me. It was on a direct course for the ford. It was going to cross the stream. It was going to the fort.

No.

The work site was just across the road, and I darted to the wheelbarrow and grabbed the best weapon I could find— a square-ended shovel. It was old and heavy, with a wood handle and a steel blade. I ran for the stream.

It had been Mouse. She'd tried to get me to stay at the fort, asked me where I was going. She and all her friends had new coats, new wood to fix the place up. She'd sold us out.

The road was littered with paralyzed bodies, and I jumped over them as I chased the four-wheeler. Iceman hadn't seen me yet. He was trying to negotiate the freshly churned mud and water. One wheel caught a rock and spun.

I never slowed. I drew back, the shovel over my shoulder

like a baseball bat, and I swung midstride. The shovel hit him squarely in the head, launching him off the ATV and into the stream. For a moment he didn't move, and by the time he did it was too late. I brought the sharp blade down on his neck. There was a bright spark as his head separated from his body. His arms and legs flailed for a moment, and then stopped.

I charged up the bank, the sound of engines still all around me. I paused at the top, hidden in the bushes.

Both trucks were there, parked at the fort, and another four-wheeler.

Becky screamed—loud for an instant, and then silence.

I ran for the door. There had to be at least three androids inside the fort, one for each vehicle. I didn't know whether I could take them all with my shovel, but I couldn't let them get Becky. I couldn't.

I'd made it to the front of the lead truck when Ms. Vaughn appeared at the gate. She saw me immediately, and drew her Taser. I was still too far away for her to get a shot, and I kept the truck between us.

Iceman came out next, Becky slung over his shoulder, as unconscious as the paralyzed students. She was bleeding from her forehead.

Ms. Vaughn called to him, and Iceman looked over at me. He dropped Becky roughly in the back of the truck, but instead of joining Ms. Vaughn in the fight he climbed in the cab and started the engine.

"No!" I shouted, and ran. Ms. Vaughn fired her Taser and missed. I dashed past her to the truck, which was backing away fast. Iceman spun the wheel, turning the truck around. He stopped for just a moment to change from reverse to drive, and I smashed the shovel into the window, shattering the glass.

Dirt flew from his tires, and the truck tore away from me.

He was down the road and in the trees in an instant.

Becky was gone.

Chapter Twenty-two

I heard Ms. Vaughn behind me, and I spun, swinging the heavy shovel. But she was too close, almost on top of me, and I hit her with only the handle, not the blade. Even so, it knocked us both off balance, and we each took a step back.

There was still no sign of the other guy from the fort, but I could hear at least one other four-wheeler behind me somewhere.

I held the shovel like an ax, one hand near the blade and one lower on the heavy handle.

She held the Taser in her right hand. She was smiling.

Maybe I should let them take me. Go wherever Becky was going, try to save her there.

No. Even if they didn't kill us, they'd put the implants in our heads. We'd be back here, trapped like everyone else. I had to find another way.

I jabbed the blade at Ms. Vaughn, and she ducked back and then immediately lunged at me. I was off guard, the long shovel hard to control, but I was able to avoid the Taser.

She lunged again, but I was ready. She was watching the

blade, so I brought the back end of the handle forward, right into her teeth.

Ms. Vaughn reeled, blood flowing from her mouth, but she didn't seem to be in any real pain.

"It's useless," she spat. "Turn yourself in."

I swung the shovel—the blade again—and she blocked it on her arm. The impact shook us both, but she didn't flinch, despite the bleeding slash in her shirtsleeve.

"I'm getting her back," I said.

"You're going to die."

"I've already killed one of your buddies."

"There are more where he came from."

"Doesn't it bother you? That you're just a duplicate?"

She laughed, cruel and evil. "Are you trying to give me some existential crisis?" The front of her shirt and neck were wet with blood.

"You're a slave."

"I enjoy what I do," she said, and lunged.

I jumped back and swung the shovel at her legs. It wasn't a great hit, but she tripped and fell down on one knee.

I didn't wait. I thrust the blunt end of the handle at her, hitting her square in the sternum. She stumbled backward, dropping the Taser and falling.

An engine roared behind me as I brought the shovel down in a killing blow. Startled, I missed her neck and plunged the shovel into her shoulder, almost severing her arm.

I looked back. Another Ms. Vaughn was twenty feet away, climbing off her ATV. She held some kind of police baton, the long metal sticks the Society kids used for security.

I snatched up the fallen Taser, stuffing it into my jacket pocket.

"Remember me?" she said.

I backed up. The shovel was still my best weapon—a much longer reach than what she had.

The wounded Ms. Vaughn also stood, her mechanical arm dangling at her side, held on by a few cables. Even with only one arm and no weapon, she advanced toward me.

"You once held a knife to my neck," the new one said. "You should have killed me when you got the chance."

Every muscle in my body seemed to ache. My ribs still burned from the fight in the forest, and I knew I couldn't hold them off much longer.

"Drop the shovel and we won't kill you," she said. It was hard to hear over the purr of the ATV behind her.

I did a quick count as they advanced on me. Two trucks and three four-wheelers. I'd killed one android, and one had left with Becky. Two were in front of me. One was still missing.

Becky got him.

I smiled. She'd kept the Taser with her. He probably opened that hole to the Basement and she'd blasted him in the face.

"What are you so happy about?"

I let the shovel answer for me, swinging it toward the wounded one in a feint, pulling up at the last second and then bringing it down like an ax onto the head of the new one. She dropped like a rock, her metal head split open around the heavy steel blade.

The wounded robot staggered, staring in surprise at her dead clone.

I yanked the shovel out of the destroyed android and turned to the other—the weakened, wounded one.

"You heard her make fun of me for not killing her when I had the chance?"

Four down. Three by me and one by Becky.

I didn't know how soon backup would come, but I made my presence known. Despite searching every android for keys, I couldn't find any for the truck, so instead I unscrewed the gas cap, stuffed in a rag soaked in lantern oil, and lit it.

I wanted to do the same to the four-wheelers, but I didn't know how much time I had. I messed with them for a minute, but eventually decided to leave.

None of the immobilized kids were waking up, which meant more androids were on the way.

I ran.

I wasn't ready for anything—to defend myself or to

escape. I needed food, and I needed the weapons, and I needed a plan.

Just as I was passing the washroom, movement by the barn caught my eye. A deer.

I dropped, pretending to be another paralyzed student.

The deer didn't look at me. It trotted down the road, coming in my direction, though it was scanning its head to the left and right. I tightened my grip on the handle of the shovel. But before the deer reached me, it turned between two of the dorms and disappeared.

I needed to hide. The Basement was compromised, I didn't want to lead anyone to the tunnel, and the forest would likely be filled with deer and raccoons soon, all robot spies.

I lifted into a crouch and ran across the road toward the ruins of the commissary. The cinder block and cement had collapsed, and the steel trusses that held up the ceiling were drooping down into the debris pile. I peered between the cracks into the dark spaces. On the far side, very near to where the elevator had been, I found what I was looking for—a cave about the size of a refrigerator. I stashed my shovel in another hole, and then squeezed into the gap. It was tight, the rough cinder block scraping my arms and face as I slid inside, and there was a danger of it collapsing further and killing me. But no one could see me, and I could wait until dark.

I wondered what was happening to Becky, what horrors she was facing. Brain surgery was the best outcome. I had to force myself to stop thinking of what else could be going on.

I didn't know what was out in the forest. There'd be more androids, certainly. More four-wheelers. Cameras, animals, sensors. I'd have to walk lightly.

No. If I went for help, then who knew what would happen to the others—to Becky. I wasn't going to go for help. I *was* the help.

A full-frontal assault. It wouldn't be subtle, but it'd be surprising.

I was going back to the school.

CHAPTER TWENTY-THREE

I didn't see anything the rest of the day—the crack in the rubble was too narrow, and it faced away from the road. There had been voices—the kids weren't paralyzed anymore—mostly hushed and nervous, and all of them too quiet to really understand. When darkness came and it felt late enough, I emerged from the hole and crept across the field to the barn.

It had snowed about two inches, and I was leaving tracks. There was nothing I could do about that. Snow here seemed to melt fast; I hoped for a warm day tomorrow.

I wore my Steelers sweatshirt now, turned inside out so the white-and-yellow logo wouldn't catch the light. In the pocket were both Tasers—the one Becky had carried so long, and the one Ms. Vaughn had dropped this morning. I knew there was another in the fort—the one Becky had used to stop Iceman—but I hadn't dared go back in for it.

I needed to get to the weapons in the tunnel.

The chickens were asleep, and hardly made any noise as

I entered the coop and lifted the filth-encrusted plywood to see the ladder.

There were plenty of supplies down here, everything Shelly had stockpiled for years—food, water, weapons— enough for the whole camp to make an escape—but no backpack.

I loaded up the best I could. I held a powerhead in each hand. I didn't want to use them yet—I wanted to save them for when I'd really need them—but I just didn't trust putting them in the front pocket of the sweatshirt. I wanted them aimed away from me.

As for the rest of the stockpile, I took a roll of thick wire, a box cutter, and a homemade weapon that looked something like an awl, but with three spikes that fit between my fingers. Just fitting it in my hand made me look forward to punching an Iceman with it.

I stood in the door of the coop, darkness and quiet all around me, and stared at the trees. I'd crossed that field not long before, carrying Becky in my arms and hoping that this town was going to be the end of my problems.

I hoisted a tarp over one shoulder, and my square-ended shovel over the other.

There had to be guards here somewhere. I peered in the windows of one of the barracks, looking for a friendly face. No one was awake. They all lay still in their beds. I wondered whether they were paralyzed tonight, so they couldn't help me.

That didn't matter. In fact, maybe it was better for me.

I crept into one of the barracks, walking down the row of beds and looking at faces in the dark.

Lily. She was here.

I searched for a pen or pencil, but found nothing. Finally, I took a piece of charcoal from the cold fireplace and scrawled a note on a T-shirt. I pulled back Lily's blanket and wrapped her fist around the shirt. She'd get the message. Whether she could do anything with it, I had no idea.

I sneaked out of the barrack, down the stairs, and then moved from shadow to shadow until I hit the tree line.

I looked back toward the town. It was too dark to see anyone, and if I was lucky no one knew I was still here, or that I was leaving. Anyone in their right mind would assume that I was running for help.

Was I in my right mind? It didn't matter. I was going anyway.

I took a breath and ran, my feet crunching against the frosted snow as I darted for the trees. There wasn't much safety there, either, but it was more than I had right now. Out there I could hide, could blend in. I could use the trees as defense and shelter. The field was a killing zone.

But no one attacked. I made it to the woods and inside,

pausing and ducking only briefly to look back and see whether I was being followed. No one. No deer, no sound of engines.

They had to be watching for me. They'd found Becky. Would they torture her to get her to talk? To tell them where I'd be hiding? The thought made me cringe—not because I was scared for myself, but because I knew her. She wouldn't give in. They'd escalate the torture, worse and worse and more and more, and she wouldn't budge. She was stronger than that, and they were going to tear her apart.

I couldn't let myself think about that. I was going to the school to stop it. I was doing all I could do.

I'd been running for at least forty-five minutes when I ducked down into a thicket and rested. I tried to listen for anyone following me, but could hardly hear the soft sounds of the forest over my own breathing.

There was nothing in these woods. It was too cold for bugs, and too dark for much else. There was hardly any wind, and I should have been able to hear the footsteps of a deer or the rustling of a raccoon. There were certainly no four-wheelers nearby. It was virtually silent.

The snow wasn't proving to be a huge problem. The pines blocked much of it, leaving only a dusting here and there, so I was able to pick a path from bare spot to bare spot.

I left the protection of the thicket and walked slower now. I guessed I was going in the right direction. I shouldn't have far to go. It had taken Becky and me all night to get from the fence to the town, but she'd been stumbling and slow, and we'd mostly been walking parallel to the wall, not directly away from it. Back at the school I'd been able to see the town's smoke from the upper floors, and it couldn't have been more than two or three miles.

But in the forest I couldn't see any landmarks—just dark trees and narrow glimpses of sky. I tried to pick out a faraway location, so I could watch it and walk toward it and stay on a somewhat straight course, but I couldn't really identify anything more than forty or fifty yards ahead.

I thought of what a tracker following me might think of my path, and smiled. Maybe I was throwing Maxfield off course without even trying.

And then I suddenly and unexpectedly felt alone—more alone than I'd ever experienced—and I had to stop. I'd always been a loner, always relied on myself, but this was different. There was no one around me—at least, I *hoped* there was no one around me now—and I could probably walk a mile or more in any direction without finding anyone. Worse, no one knew where I was. Not the school or the other kids or Becky or anyone. No one had any idea.

But that wasn't the real problem. After all, I'd spent my entire life with no one knowing where I was. I'd been in a city, surrounded by people on every street corner and alley, but they'd never *cared* where I was—that was the whole reason I'd been brought to Maxfield Academy in the first place. Everyone in the school was picked because no one would miss them.

And that was the difference: someone was wondering where I was, wishing I was there and relying on me. Becky was somewhere, probably in pain, or on an operating table getting an implant in her brain, and she wanted me there.

I was alone, and someone missed me. And that hurt worse than just being alone.

I hurried off, jogging again, avoiding any brush or loose rock that might make a sound. I couldn't go fast—it was too dark, and my goal was too important to risk a sprained ankle—but I moved as quickly as I could.

Back and forth, fifty yards forward, twenty yards to the side, ten yards back at a diagonal, and then fifty yards forward again. I had to hurry, but I wasn't going to get caught.

It was still dark when I got to the fence. I wouldn't have seen it—it was almost invisible in the darkness—but the wide swaths of cleared ground on both sides gave it away. As I approached I could almost hear the hum of the electricity running through the steel.

I didn't want to cut anything—I didn't know how the fence worked, and cutting the wrong thing and breaking the circuit could alert the school that someone was there. Or it could kill me. Instead, I was going to climb.

Twenty minutes of searching produced a perfect log: dead and dry, about fifteen feet long and lined with broken branches like thorns on the stem of a rose—essentially a ready-made ladder. I couldn't find another like it, but all I needed now was something to stabilize it, and two shorter logs did the trick. I leaned the long one up and over the fence, pressing down into the mass of razor wire, and then braced it with the others.

I climbed the log, inching up from one dead branch to the next. It wobbled, and the fence shook, the chain link ringing against the steel posts. Up close now, the fence only inches from me, I could feel the electricity in the air, hear it hissing.

The farther up I got, the more the log bowed and creaked.

I paused and checked my balance so I could stand securely without hands. Then, carefully and slowly, I pulled the tarp from my shoulder. It was heavy canvas, and coated with something to waterproof it. I hoped it was as tough as it looked.

I let it unroll, hanging down from my precarious perch. I'd been carrying it for hours, but the weight now seemed daunting. I wanted to throw it over the razor wire like a blanket over a bed, but it was heavy and awkward. I had to pull it back, fold it roughly in half, and then push it over the coils of sharp metal. It wasn't pretty, and it was liable to slide off, but I didn't need much time.

As I put my weight on it, the razor wire flexed and bounced beneath me. There was no substance there, and I worried I'd fall into the center of the spool instead of climb over it. But a moment later my hand felt the steel crossbar of the fence under the tarp.

I crawled over, and in an instant the springy coils flexed apart and I tumbled down through a mess of shredded canvas. I hit the ground on the other side with a thud, in a splash of snow, and my old injuries flared in pain. But I was over.

The tarp was hanging on the wire, and a few tugs proved it wasn't going anywhere. It was snagged in a dozen places, sharp razors poking through new holes.

The whole scene left a lot to be desired. If anyone monitored this fence they couldn't miss this huge mess. It was obvious what had happened here.

That made time all the more important.

I'd done the rest of this before. I knew the wall was close, and I knew how to cross it. There'd be cameras there, and I knew I would have to be more watchful for the school's animals, but my chest swelled with confidence. I'd made it this far. I was going to make it the rest of the way.

Chapter Twenty-Four

The snow was falling heavier when I got to the wall, sticking to my sweatshirt in big white flakes the size of cotton balls. There were cameras here, as I'd expected, and I stayed in the cover of the forest as I looked for a flaw in the security. There was a camera about every hundred feet, aimed at the top of the wall, not at the ground.

It wasn't like it mattered too much. My entire goal was to get sent to detention. But that was just it: I needed to get inside the school and go down into the underground complex through the detention elevator. All of the maps were created by people who went that way, and if I got caught out here then I might be hauled off somewhere else—to whatever entrance they used to get to the trucks.

So I needed to avoid the cameras.

I stood and pondered for a long time before finally deciding on a course of action. I couldn't knock the cameras out of the way—whoever was monitoring them would notice that one had been moved. I couldn't climb over the top of the camera, because each camera watched over the next one.

My final tactic was lousy, but it was going to have to do.

I darted across the open ground, hoping the falling snow would help hide me. I hit the base of the wall, flattening myself against it.

I was directly under a camera.

I felt stupid as I tried to block its view, like a little kid throwing snowballs at a stop sign. I figured that unless the guard was watching the camera at all times, they wouldn't realize that the snow on the lens didn't come from the blowing storm.

It took a dozen tries before I got a direct hit, obscuring about two-thirds of the lens. It would have to do.

Five minutes later I was over it, using the same log trick I'd used at the fence. It was amazing how much easier it was to get over the wall when a gang with a security contract wasn't chasing me down. And when I was trying to break *into* prison, instead of out.

I ran deep into the woods, away from the cameras.

I was back. I'd fought so hard to get out of this place—but it felt strangely like home. When I ducked under the weathered pink ribbons that marked the paintball fields, I couldn't help but feel a little nostalgic. I was trapped back then, sure, but I'd had my friends with me. I was part of a group. This time I was on my own.

The path was easy now, but I walked it slowly, watching on all sides for animals. It was morning—if the snow hadn't been falling, the sun would have been up. Students in the school were probably waking up and taking showers. I wondered what they'd think when I showed up.

I could see the building, a dark mass surrounded by white lawns and trees and sky. I'd been gone for a week, but it felt so much longer.

Moving from tree to tree, I made my way to the front of the school. There was less brush here, so I had to hide deeper inside the forest—about forty feet—at the base of a short limestone outcropping.

Getting inside was going to be harder than climbing a wall. The windows here were bulletproof, and the doors could be opened only by someone with the right contract.

I could run up to the doors, bang on them, and hope that whoever heard me had the ability to let me in. But if Maxfield saw me approach, I'd never make it.

I pulled my legs up to my chest. It was cold, and I was getting wetter every minute. The snow sticking to my clothes was melting now, and I had begun to shiver. I stuffed my hands inside my sleeves and pulled up my hood. It could be a long wait.

With nothing else to do, I overprepared. I rolled up my pant legs and used the wire to tie the powerheads to my shins. I had to hide the weapons so I could make it down the detention elevator still armed. The powerheads made me nervous. If I fell, would I shoot off my own foot?

I hid the box cutter in my shoe. There was no place to conceal the Tasers, so I kept them in my sweatshirt.

My fingers were starting to seize up. Too cold.

I saw a face. Across the lawn of the school, in the bank of windows above the front door, someone was peering out. It was hard to be sure—it was far away, and the windows were a little cloudy—but it looked like a girl. Long dark hair.

Red sweater, white collar. The Maxfield uniform.

She was staring, hands on the glass. I knew she couldn't see me—I was well hidden and covered in snow—but she just stood there and stared.

Another student appeared beside her. They weren't looking at each other—they were looking outside.

A few minutes later a third person came, and then another.

I knew this. Faces in the windows, watching and waiting. It was the first thing I ever saw when I got here.

They were expecting a car.

I gripped the shovel beside me, which was entirely covered in snow now. This was my chance.

Twenty minutes passed, and then thirty. By the time I heard an engine, the windows were filled with faces. They were waiting to warn the new students not to leave the car, not to come inside. But something else was happening, too—I kept thinking of those two sisters. They went to the underground complex, had surgery, but never came to the town. Harvard said he saw them in the school. And Curtis had seen people who were kidnapped. Things were different now. The school had changed its procedures.

I rose up into a crouch, one freezing hand gripping the shovel. I was debating between that and the Tasers, but the shovel had been so useful before.

The car appeared off to my right, moving slowly on the unplowed, unmarked road. It was a large sedan, one driver in the front, two passengers in the back.

I wanted to run up to meet it. I wanted to kill another incarnation of Ms. Vaughn. But I didn't dare move until that school door was open. I couldn't risk Maxfield locking the building down.

The car slowed to a stop. The driver stepped out. Ms. Vaughn again, this time wearing a business suit. She opened the back door and leaned inside.

The first person stepped out. A boy. Short, maybe thirteen or fourteen. He was wearing a bright red T-shirt and shorts. He was in handcuffs. That was different.

The second climbed out through the same door. Another boy, a little older. It looked like he was in pajamas. He had on handcuffs, too. They both looked terrified, but didn't know what to do. They were captives, in the middle of nowhere, in a blizzard.

Ms. Vaughn stood in front of them, gesturing. I remembered her telling me how much I'd love it here, but these kids already knew it was a prison. She was probably threatening them, not reassuring them. A moment later she was in her car, the doors closed, and she began to drive. The boys watched her go, one of them already heading cautiously up the stairs and out of the falling snow.

I was ignoring the car now, my eyes glued on that door.

The other kid took a tentative step up.

The faces in the window were waving their arms in warning.

The door opened.

I jumped up, snow falling from my clothes as I sprinted out of the trees and across the snowy lawn. No one seemed to notice.

A girl appeared in the doorway. Red sweater, white shirt, gray skirt. For a moment I thought she actually was Becky.

One of the boys saw me, his handcuffed arms raised as he pointed me out to the other.

I glanced to the road. Ms. Vaughn's car was out of sight.

I was almost to them now. The younger boy backed away, and the other called to me for help.

The girl stepped back, her hand gripping the door nervously.

"Don't," I bellowed, my voice dry and harsh.

There was fear in her eyes, but I was close now.

"Gabby!" I shouted. "Don't close it. I'm here to help."

The shovel wasn't going to do me any good inside—there

wouldn't be enough room to swing it—so I dropped it on the stairs and pulled the Tasers from the pocket of my sweatshirt. I held one in each hand.

I took the steps two at a time. Gabby—the dupe—had no idea who I was, only that I knew her name. Her eyes were wide, but she was frozen in place. That was all I needed.

A moment later I was past her, inside the ornate front entry. I held out the Tasers like pistols, turning in a circle, watching for guards.

"Who are you?" she asked, her voice tiny. She was still standing on the top step, holding the door.

"This is all fake," I said, checking the stairs and peeking down the corridor. "Half the people in this school aren't real."

Gabby didn't answer.

No one was coming. I needed to get sent to detention, but I had no idea how the security contracts worked now, or whether there even were contracts. I stepped back to the door. I regretted what I was about to do, but I knew she wasn't real—she was a robot. Gabby was back in the town.

I stuffed one of the Tasers into my pocket and pulled her back inside, grabbed her by the jaw, and shoved her against the wall. She began to shake, but that was exactly what I wanted. I needed her to be scared. I held the Taser up, inches from her face, and pulled the trigger, electricity popping and cracking. She closed her eyes, trying to turn away.

"No," I shouted, shaking her. "Look at me. Look at me!"

One eye slowly opened. Her whole body was trembling, but she wasn't fighting.

"I'm inside, Gabby," I said. "Tell the others I'm inside. Tell Lily it's time."

She began to cry, and I let go of her.

There were voices on the stairs. I drew the second Taser again, and began backing up toward the basement.

"It's all fake," I shouted. "This school is run by robots."

I must have sounded like a lunatic.

I kept waiting for Gabby to pop, for Maxfield to take her over and attack me, but she didn't.

She couldn't. All the new humans had just arrived. If they immediately saw one of their own revealed as a robot, the school would turn to chaos.

There were footsteps somewhere, the squeak of sneakers on marble.

I spun, trying to see which hall it came from.

"Gabby, Curtis, Carrie, Shelly, Harvard, Mouse—they're not real," I said. "They're fake. They're robots. Tapti, Eliana, Walnut . . ." I listed as many names as I could remember from the town. I didn't know what good it would do. All I wanted was for someone to send me to detention or for Ms. Vaughn came back.

"We know," someone said, and I looked up the stairs to

see a boy I vaguely recognized. Not from school, but from the outside world.

A blond-haired girl appeared next to him, and then another. They looked almost identical. The sisters.

I recognized them instantly.

They were the daughters of the president of the United States. I stared—too long.

Lights exploded all around me, and I was on my face on the marble. Both Tasers flew from my hands, skittering across the smooth stone.

I rolled onto my back just in time for someone huge— Curtis!—to grab for my hands. I kicked him, driving my heel into his knee, and he fell.

"Get him!" Curtis yelled.

Finally.

I scrambled to my feet. Skiver and Walnut were thundering on the stairs, chasing me.

I needed to make it look like a mistake. I ran, pretending I didn't know where I should go, and then darted down to the basement.

I didn't want them to catch me until I was there—I didn't want to give them a reason to search me. They just needed to throw me in detention and close the door.

The only weapon I had accessible was the fist spikes, and as I ran I fitted them into my hand. Three heavy nails, each protruding two inches past my fingers when I clenched my fist.

I could hear them running after me as we turned down the final corridor. The ceiling was low here, and the walls narrow. It was old concrete, and it smelled damp. I ran past door after door—empty, dark storage rooms—and finally turned to face them. I was maybe twenty feet from the detention elevator.

"You're not real," I said, smiling.

"Dude's gone crazy," Walnut said, the more nervous of the two.

Skiver kept coming, unarmed. I wondered whether he could tell my fist wasn't just a fist.

"Skiver, I know you can see me," I said, talking to the human. "This one's for you."

I lunged at the robot, my fist connecting with his gut. He shrieked as the spikes stabbed him, and he stared at me, his face contorted in pain. Walnut backed up, finally seeing I was armed.

"What?" Skiver stammered, holding his stomach.

And then he was gone. The pain disappeared from his face and he stepped toward me, completely unafraid. Skiver had popped.

I swung at him again, and he blocked my fist with his arm, the vicious spears gouging into his forearm. He ignored them and slammed me in the chest with the heel of his hand. I fell backward. It felt like he'd hit me with a hammer.

I gasped for breath. I'd lost the spikes now, too, and I scrambled away, trying to get back on my feet.

There was no time. The robot Skiver was on top of me, his fingers around my neck. He picked me up with one hand then threw me backward again. I didn't have time to do anything. I couldn't breathe. I couldn't move.

He grabbed my shoulder, and I thought his fingers and thumb were going to tear into my flesh, shatter my collarbone.

In one swift movement he threw me sideways. I expected to hit a wall, but I passed through a door, crashing onto a hard linoleum floor.

I tried to defend myself, only to see that he wasn't coming any closer. He was framed in a doorway. He pulled the door closed, locking me in the dark.

Silence.

The room heaved.

I was going down.

CHAPTER TWENTY-FIVE

My Tasers were gone, and the fist spikes. I rolled up my pants and untied the powerheads. They both seemed to be fine, though I had no idea whether they'd work. Still, I liked holding them—they felt substantial in my hands, the grip of the screwdrivers heavy and comfortable.

I still had the box cutter in my shoe, but decided against pulling it out for now. The door could open at any minute, and I didn't want to be shoeless.

The room lurched and stopped. The lights dimmed for an instant, and then came back.

I faced the door, suddenly terrified.

There had been blood on this floor before, Becky once told me. Not everyone who got sent to detention just gave up and went to surgery. They fought back, right here, and they died.

Click.

Someone was messing with the door. Unlocking it.

I crouched.

There was a sliver of bright light as the door creaked open.

I took a cautious step forward.

No sounds.

I reached my foot out and kicked the door the rest of the way open.

The hallway was wide here. Androids could be hiding on either side. They probably figured I was armed, so it made sense that they'd set a trap.

I stared down the length of the hall. It was brighter than I imagined, the walls white tile and plaster, and lit with exposed lightbulbs every five or six feet. It reminded me of an old hospital. There was a chemical smell, like harsh soap.

"You're dead," I said.

No answer.

If there was someone there, they'd expect me to jump out and attack. That's what they were prepared for. So that wasn't what I was going to do.

I took a breath, as deep as I could. And then I ran.

In an instant I was out the door and pounding down the hall.

At fifty feet I spun around.

Two of them, both Iceman. One, dressed in workman's coveralls, had a metal baton. The other, wearing medical scrubs, held a Taser in his hand—it had been fired, the probes and wires lying tangled on the floor. He'd missed me as I ran.

He ripped off the cartridge and approached me now.

My hands were sweaty, and I suddenly worried about holding on to the powerheads.

"Please do not resist," the workman said.

"Did you hear what I did to the others?" I said. "I killed four of you."

The workman smiled as they continued toward me. "Death does not scare us."

"Then why didn't you come in that door to get me?"

I needed to do something soon. My back was to an open hallway. Someone could sneak up behind me anytime.

"Where's Becky?"

"Perfectly safe. As you will be when you surrender."

They were close now, maybe eight feet away.

"You already know about Fort Maxfield," the workman said. "You know that we don't kill or torture."

"I'm not going back there."

"Yes, you are."

"Where's Becky?"

The man in scrubs lunged at me, the face of the Taser sparking white and blue. I smacked his arm away with my left, but the powerhead in that hand flew out of my fingers, clattering down the hall.

He was almost on top of me, and I brought the other

powerhead up, stabbing into his ribs.

Bang!

Everything stopped.

The noise exploded down the hall, and the shock made us both startle and stagger backward. The spent powerhead dropped from my fingers.

He had a bloody hole in his chest, a ring of torn skin and cloth around shattered circuits and machinery.

He looked at me and fell.

I jumped back to my feet. The workman looked stunned, staring at his dead partner.

I picked up the Taser. "Still not afraid of death?"

The workman jumped, swinging the baton like an ax. But the ceiling was too low, and it skittered against the cement, smashing a lightbulb and coming down harmlessly a foot away from me.

I leapt past him, running for the second powerhead. He was right behind me.

The baton swiped past my ear, the tip scraping pain-lessly down my shoulder as I dropped to grab the weapon. I snatched it off the ground, turned to him, and jammed the barrel into his stomach.

The powerhead bent in half, the barrel ripping off to the side and snapping off, leaving me holding only a screw-driver.

He didn't wait, but crashed the baton into my arm. Pain

shot from my fingertips to my shoulder. I dropped the Taser and screamed.

The workman advanced mercilessly, pushing me back toward the elevator. I didn't have any good weapons left—just the screwdriver and the box cutter in my shoe. There'd be no time to get it.

"Tell me where she is and I'll let you go," I said.

He didn't respond—not a word or an expression. He continued walking, and I kept retreating.

I glanced back. Nothing could help me. The door to the detention room, the elevator controls, a lightbulb. Nothing.

He swiped the baton again, but just to scare me. He knew he had me cornered.

But I was cornered only if I was going to stay underground.

I turned and ran, jamming the button for the elevator to go up.

I heard his footsteps behind me. I knew he wouldn't let me go. He wasn't trying to hit me now—he was trying to get inside that elevator before it left.

As soon as I got inside I spun, slamming the door into him. It caught on his shoulder and arm, and he reeled.

I rammed the screwdriver into his chest.

Whether it was his artificial heart or the power system Harvard had mentioned, it didn't matter. He dropped.

I jumped back out into the hallway and shoved his body

the rest of the way inside. I closed the door and let the elevator leave, taking the body of a dead robot up to the students.

I was dripping with sweat, my heart pumping so hard I could feel it in my neck, arms, and fingers. But I didn't have time to catch my breath. Backup was sure to be coming.

I grabbed the Taser and stared down the hall, trying to visualize the map again. I needed to get to the cells.

I ran.

There was no one in the corridors. No one in the rooms to my sides. I'd killed six androids in the last week, and Becky had likely Tasered a seventh. Maybe they were running out.

I turned the corner to the cell block. The lights were on, but dim. Curtis was right—it looked like a hospital, with a nurses' station and everything.

I crept in, but couldn't walk quietly. My clothes were still soaking wet from the heavy snow, and my shoes squeaked on the tile floor.

Every room was the same: a bed and a sink and a toilet. They all had prison bars, and instead of a keyhole there was a ten-digit keypad. Those pads were the only thing in the entire cell block that looked less than fifty years old.

My heart was in my throat as I hurried down the row. I passed two dozen rooms, and a junction that led to another hallway, before I found her.

I gripped the bars and stared.

Becky was unconscious, a bandage around her head and a plastic mask covering her nose and mouth. A wheeled cart was beside her bed, and all the tubes, wires, and sensors covering her body ran to it. It hissed as she breathed.

They'd done the surgery. They must have.

Other than that, she didn't appear hurt. She was wearing a T-shirt and a pair of shorts, and her arms and legs all looked perfectly undamaged. Her bicep was fully healed. Only a wide, faint scar was visible. Even the frost nip on her chin and nose were gone, leaving perfect, healthy skin.

I reached my arm in, trying to squeeze through the bars. To touch her. But she was six inches too far. My fingertips could reach the cart, and for a moment I thought I could use it to pull her toward me, but that wouldn't work. It would just pull the equipment off her.

I ran back to the nurses' station, wildly throwing open drawers and cabinets. The code for the keypad had to be somewhere. But all I found were rolls of bandage and tape and more of those foil sheets Jane had used. Whatever that stuff was, it would be worth billions in the free world, but it was as good as garbage to me here.

"Having trouble?"

I turned, holding out the Taser at Ms. Vaughn. She was standing at the hallway door, apparently unarmed. She wore a business suit. I wondered whether she was the same Ms. Vaughn I'd seen outside, dropping off the new kids.

"Let her out," I said, but even I could hear the fear in my own voice. Ms. Vaughn stepped into the room, not threatening, not preparing for an attack. Just casual, like we were friends.

I shook the Taser at her. "Don't come any closer."

"What are you going to do?" she said. "You came here for her, and you can't get her. You've lost."

I backed up, cautiously moving to Becky's cell. Ms. Vaughn followed.

Was there a way I could get her to open the cell?

A second android appeared behind her—another Ms. Vaughn, this one in scrubs, like the Iceman I'd killed. She didn't appear to be armed either.

I focused back on the businesswoman.

"Are you out of guards?" I asked. "You don't look dressed for a fight."

She raised her eyebrows. "Were you going to fight?"

I was at Becky's room again, and I glanced inside. I still had no idea how to make them go in there.

"Give up," she said, and reached into her jacket.

No Taser this time. It was a gun. The same make and model as the .38 that Maxfield had once given Isaiah. "We use Tasers because you students are valuable to us," she said. "But I think you're more trouble than you're worth."

I had no options. There was nowhere to run. I was captured, and I couldn't save her.

Becky's breathing was deep and loud as the ventilator on her face gave her oxygen. It was the only sound in the hall.

I moved to Becky's cell bars.

The businesswoman laughed. "You don't have to take a bullet for your girlfriend. She's never been as much trouble as you. Besides, she's already had surgery—we'd hate to waste it."

That was what I was counting on.

I took a breath, and then turned my back to the android, reaching between the bars. My fingers were so close.

Someone grabbed my shoulder. I dropped the Taser and held myself against the bars, stretching.

My middle finger caught the cart, and the rest of my fingertips, and then my whole hand.

"Benson," Ms. Vaughn shouted, yanking me back.

I let her. My hand was tight on the cart.

I flew backward, tossed by the businesswoman's robotic strength. The cart followed, crashing into the bars when it could go no farther.

An alarm sounded, and despite the gun in my face I craned my neck to see Becky, to pray she was okay.

All the sensors and tubes had pulled from her body, and I could see she was fighting for air.

The woman in scrubs yelled at me. "You came this far just to kill her!" And she jumped past us to the bars. To the keypad.

6-5-6-3-8. *Buzz. Click.*

The bars popped open, and she was inside, checking the cart and pulling it back beside Becky's bed.

"It's over, Benson," Ms. Vaughn said. And then she hit me with the butt of the gun.

CHAPTER TWENTY-SIX

I woke in the dark. It took a long time, a fight for consciousness against whatever chemicals were pumping through
my body. People came and went. They asked me questions,
and I think I answered them, but all of those conversations
were lost to me now.

I was in a hospital bed, but the back was propped up so
I could see everything in the room. The same white tiles
were on the floor and halfway up the walls, and then it was
concrete the rest of the way.

The room smelled like nothing. No soap, no must, nothing.

One of my eyes didn't open all the way, but I felt no pain.
I tried to touch it.

My hands were bound with thick leather restraints. My
ankles, too.

"Mr. Fisher. You're awake."

I turned to look, but could see no one.

It was a male voice, but it didn't sound like Iceman.

"Who are you?"

"You've caused me a lot of trouble, Mr. Fisher." The sound was tinny, like it was coming from a microphone.

Or my ears weren't working right. Or I was imagining it.

"Are you Maxfield?"

The voice chuckled, deep and warbling, like an old man's. When he spoke he sounded like he had too much saliva in his mouth. "There's no Maxfield. It's a name. It could have been anything."

"What do you want?"

"Does it matter what I want? I'm here to discuss what you want."

"You know what I want."

"Do I?" he asked. "You change your mind a lot. When you first came to my academy, you only wanted your freedom. But soon your freedom wasn't enough. You wanted freedom for everybody."

"What do you care?"

"Now I'm not sure what to think. You aren't concerned about everybody anymore. You're only concerned about one person. Rebecca Allred."

"Where is she?"

"Why do you keep shouting?" he asked. "I can hear you perfectly."

I fought against the restraints. There had to be some way out of this.

"I'm not in the practice of negotiating, Mr. Fisher," he

said tiredly. "I have gotten used to being in control. So it saddens me that things have come to this."

I stopped pulling against the leather bands, panting, and listened.

"They say you should never begin negotiations without being prepared, without knowing your alternatives to an agreement. What, Mr. Fisher, are your alternatives to a negotiated agreement?"

I didn't answer. I wasn't sure what he was talking about.

"I'll help you out," he said, condescension dripping from his voice. "Your alternative to negotiation is that I kill you. On the other hand, if you do negotiate, I'll let you live in Fort Maxfield as part of the program."

"The program?"

"The program," he said. "You're very familiar with the program."

I didn't want to talk about this. "Where's Becky?"

"Ah, yes. That's another part of the negotiation, isn't it? You can save her or kill her, too. I'm only telling you this so that you know what you're dealing with. You always want the town or the academy to be more fair, so I'm being fair. I'm telling you the rules."

I was trapped and talking to a madman. "Why are you doing this?" I shouted.

He ignored me. "Now that you know the ground rules and the outcomes, let's negotiate. You know something that I would like to know."

"This isn't a negotiation," I said. "This is threatening me for information."

He laughed, wet and guttural. "All negotiations are threats. Every negotiation says, 'Agree to this or there will be a consequence.'"

I rubbed my head on the pillow, trying to tell whether I had a bandage. Had they done surgery on me? I didn't feel anything.

"Well?" he asked.

"Well, what?"

"You have information that you're hiding from me."

"What do you want to know?" I yelled. "Walnut always takes more than his share of dessert. Harvard takes long showers and uses up all the hot water. Gabby—"

He cut me off, his voice suddenly sharp and harsh. "Tell me where the students are."

I paused. The note I'd left for Lily had worked: to hide as many students as she could in the tunnel and stay there. If it was true that the implants couldn't track them down there, then Maxfield would have no idea where they'd gone. It was my bargaining chip.

"Which students?"

"Don't play with me."

"No, really," I said. "I don't know which students."

"Lilian Paterson, Curtis Shaw, Caroline Flynn, Michelle

Bowers . . . Need I go on? The list is quite extensive."

I smiled.

"So you do know where they are," the voice said.

"I assume they escaped," I answered. "Good for them."

There was silence for a moment.

"I'm going to make a slight concession," he said. "And pay close attention, because this is the only one I'm going to make. And it's what you call a limited-time offer."

I waited. I knew he wasn't going to offer anything I'd accept. I hadn't come this far to not finish.

"You and Ms. Allred are protected," he said. "You do not have to stay in the town. I'll have a small house built for you elsewhere on the property. You won't have to worry about the other students—the gangs and the fighting. You can live your lives there and be happy."

I could see it, and for an instant it sounded perfect. It wasn't freedom, but it was comfort. And I'd be with her.

He continued before I could answer. "I want you to know that she's listening. She's here with me."

"Let me talk to her."

"A negotiation is based on trust," he said with a chuckle.

"The answer is no," I said. "If she is there with you, and if you'd let her talk, she'd say the same thing."

"Mr. Fisher—"

"You can go to hell, you son of a bitch."

There was silence. For a moment I thought he was gone,

but I could hear faint breathing.

"I'll give you some time to think," he said. "The offer is still on the table. For a limited time."

The voice was gone. An instant later, the lights went out, leaving me in the dark. Something behind me glowed faintly blue, reflecting on the glassy tile.

I wondered whether she really had been listening. It didn't matter. Neither of us could have agreed to that. It wasn't about freedom anymore. For her it was about saving the others. For me it was knowing I'd have a lifetime of guilt. Maybe there was some nobility trapped in there somewhere. I didn't know.

The voice didn't come back for a long time. I fell asleep again, and I woke up to the sharp stick of a needle.

Ms. Vaughn stood beside my bed, a dimly lit shadow, injecting something into my arm.

"Truth serum?" I asked.

"Breakfast," she answered.

And then she was gone. I didn't know whether that was truth or a mind game.

I slept again.

I dreamed about the first time I'd seen Becky, stepping out the front door of the school and welcoming me with a warm, optimistic grin. She'd dressed like the Society then, with too much makeup and her brown hair molded with finger waves. She was beautiful.

I reached for her, but as I stretched out my arm she got farther and farther away, the stairs of the school multiplying into a mountain between us. As she got smaller, more distant, an arm—a tentacle—snaked out of the door, pulling her back inside. She screamed, and I screamed.

Suddenly I was awake, shaking in my bed and fighting the restraints.

The lights came on, and they felt like floodlights. I smashed my eyes shut and turned my head away.

"Good evening, Benson," the voice said. "Have you thought about my offer?"

"The answer is still no."

"They can't have disabled the implants," the voice said. "Do I need to raze the entire town?"

"Maybe they escaped while I was distracting you."

"Impossible."

"Maybe we're smarter than you think we are."

"You're smart, Benson, but you're not that smart."

"If I tell you—" I stopped myself. I was going to say that if I told him then I'd have no more leverage—that as soon as I told him, he had no reason to keep his promises.

I couldn't believe I'd almost said it.

"If you tell me what?"

"Nothing."

"You're not looking well, Benson," he said.

"You're trying to wear me down."

He laughed. "I am wearing you down."

"The answer is still no," I repeated.

"Then make a counter! I'm here to negotiate. What will it take?"

"Let everyone go. Shut down the school."

He guffawed—a loud, long belly laugh. "I don't want to know that much."

"No," I said. "I think you want to know. The longer you wait, the closer they get to civilization and rescue. Time's ticking for you."

"I repeat," he said, his voice perfectly calm, "you can't have disabled the implants."

"Why are the president's daughters in the school?" I asked, trying to put him on the defensive.

"That should be the least of your concerns."

"Who are you?"

The lights went out, but an image appeared on the wall in front of me, projected from somewhere over my head.

Becky.

I could feel panic rising in my chest, and I fought against the restraints.

She sat alone in her cell, her hands behind her back, her legs tied to the chair. Her face and T-shirt were wet with sweat.

"She's a pretty little thing, isn't she?" the voice said. Becky's head popped up at the sound of the voice.

"We're all on a party line," he said. "So maybe you ought to say hello."

"Becky?"

"Bense?"

"We're going to get out of here," I told her, and felt tears coming down my face.

The voice cut in. "You certainly are. Becky, Benson here hasn't been telling me what I want to know."

She was looking up, toward the sound. It didn't look like she was seeing an image of me.

"Maybe you should tell Benson to spill the beans."

"Benson," she called, "where are you?"

"I'm okay," I said. "We're going to get out of here."

"I don't even know what he's talking about," she said. "What secret?"

I didn't answer—I couldn't.

"He won't free everyone," I said.

She nodded.

My words hung there. She wasn't arguing, but she didn't have to, because I was arguing with myself now. Of course he wouldn't free anyone. He was right—he knew the students couldn't have left the perimeter. I didn't have bargaining power.

"Benson," the voice said. "You can put a stop to this."

I was about to ask what, but another person appeared in the projection. Iceman, walking up behind her.

Becky saw him, too, and squirmed in her chair.

Iceman flipped open a knife—short and curved and vicious.

"Stop!" I yelled. "What the hell are you doing?"

"I tried to offer you the carrot," the voice said. "This is the stick."

As he said the last word, Iceman jabbed the knife into her hand.

She screamed—high and terrified and desperate.

The projection disappeared and the lights came back up.

"Let her go," I yelled, flailing in the bed. "Leave her alone."

"You intrigue me," he said calmly.

"What's going on? What's he doing to her?"

"I'm going to have to revise my assessment of you, Benson. The last time we talked, I'd guessed you cared the most about her, but now I don't know what to think."

"Of course I do," I blurted, fire raging throughout my body. "I just don't trust you."

"You're afraid I won't follow through on my promise?"

"No."

"What do you want? Shall I drive you and Becky to the little house in the forest and leave you there, and you can mail me the information I want?"

"I don't even think that was the real Becky," I said, gesturing to the wall with my head.

He paused. "What do you mean?"

"You're torturing her," I said, "but what if you're torturing a robot? How am I supposed to know? I saw that Becky already has the implant."

He paused again, and his voice was more thoughtful now. "If you'd like, I can fillet her arm, like all you barbarians did at the fort."

"That can be faked," I said. He was showing me a projection. It could all be computers. It could be a newer model of android.

"It can?"

"Go to hell."

The lights went out.

It was happening too fast, too out of control. I didn't know what I was doing anymore. Was I protecting her more by being quiet or talking?

I shouldn't be forced to make this decision. Why did I have to choose? What made me responsible for getting everyone in that town to safety? Because I was the only one without an implant in my head? That didn't make me a leader—it just made me slightly luckier.

But that knife in Becky's hand. Her scream. It pushed everything else out of my mind, and in the darkness I couldn't see anything on that wall but her. In pain.

Chapter Twenty-Seven

I woke up, so I must have been asleep.

An alarm sounded, and a light somewhere behind me flashed. It lasted for minutes. Hours. I didn't know. And then it turned off.

I'd been in that bed for days—maybe weeks. I couldn't tell.

I listened for the voice, but heard only the whir of some distant fan.

And a scratch. Something scratched something.

I turned my head.

Was it a mouse? Was it Ms. Vaughn?

Was I going crazy?

There it was again, only it wasn't a scratch. It was a scrape. It was something moving, sliding, brushing on the floor.

Was someone sneaking up behind me?

The bed vibrated—hardly noticeable, but I knew something had bumped it.

"Who's there?"

"Shh."

I turned to the noise, and saw Becky's face at the side of the bed. She was grinning, her finger to her lips.

I felt like I was melting, like water had crashed over me and swept every other thought from my head. She was here, next to me. She was undoing the restraint on my arm.

"How did you . . . ?"

She looked awful—hair wet and matted, and her face streaked with dried tears. I wanted to kiss her. Wanted to hug her and never let go.

"I told you," she whispered. "I grew up on a ranch. I made a rabbit trap."

She undid the first strap, and I pulled my hand free. Every muscle in my arm felt weak and sore. I grabbed her hand and looked at it. No scar.

"You weren't hurt?"

Becky's face went dark, and she kind of bobbed her head. I didn't know what that meant, but the smooth skin on the back of her hand didn't lie. The girl in the projection wasn't her. I'd been right.

She moved to my foot, and I used my free hand to pry the leather off my left. It was almost impossible—it needed two hands, and my one was too cramped and aching to be much good anyway.

"What were they doing to you?" she whispered, unlatching my right foot and moving to my left. I pulled up my leg, flexing the unused muscles.

"Trying to get me to talk. Are there guards in the halls?"

She shook her head. "Talk about what?"

She unlatched the left foot.

"I'm so glad to see you," I said. As she came to my left side and bent by my arm, I touched her face. "I'm glad you're okay."

Becky smiled, tilting her face into my hand for a moment before mouthing a quick, happy, *Wait*, and focusing again on the restraint.

"Were they asking about the weapons?" she whispered. "Where we got the bullets?"

"No."

She squeezed the latch out and released the leather strap. "Then what?"

I swung my legs over the side of the bed and stood. My legs wobbled, and Becky reached to steady me.

I didn't want to wait any longer. I wrapped my arms around her, pulling her close against me.

This wasn't how I had pictured our first real kiss. But I needed to do it.

I cupped her face in my hands, our lips meeting softly, but then she pressed into me and I pulled her even closer.

I needed her to know how I felt, how I missed her. How I loved her.

Her fingers tugged at my hair as she kissed my lips, my face, my neck.

I held her, my hands running up her sides. Feeling her ribs, her armpit. The small, unnatural knot under the skin.

"Becky," I said, grabbing her face and looking into her eyes. "I love you."

She giggled and said something, but I didn't care what it was. She wasn't Becky. She was a camera.

"I love you," I said. "You're going to be okay. The code for the keypad is six-five-six-three-eight."

She frowned. "What are you talking about?"

"Go for the control room," I said, staring into her eyes. "I'll meet you there."

She froze.

We stared at each other for just an instant, and then her hands—which had been running through my hair—jumped to my throat.

But she didn't have time. There wasn't much strength left in me, but I smashed my fist into her armpit. The system sheared, her artificial heart too close to the power supply.

She dropped like a stone.

Chapter Twenty-Eight

I ran down the stark white halls, trying to orient myself. I hadn't seen them take me to this room, so I had no real idea where I was.

An alarm was sounding again, small red bulbs flashing on and off about every fifty feet, but I had yet to see anyone.

I turned a corner, and then another. Every hallway looked the same.

I flung a door open, hoping to find something I recognized, but it was just full of boxes. The next one had dozens of what looked like computer servers, a million flashing lights and glowing cables, but I didn't know enough about technology to be sure.

Someone was at the end of the hallway, and for a moment I thought it was Becky, but no—it was a Ms. Vaughn. I turned and ran the other way.

Nothing was familiar—or, rather, everything was familiar. It all looked the same, every hall and every door.

I turned a corner and was almost bowled over by Becky.

"Bense!" She grabbed me in a bear hug, and I pushed her

back, pointing down the hall at Ms. Vaughn.

"It'll have to wait," I said, holding her hand as we ran.

"It'll be worth it."

She steered me through the halls—the maps had shown us how to get to the control room from the cell block, so she knew where she was.

I had bare feet—so did she—and pain shot up my heels and calves as I pounded down the hard tile floors. I hurt everywhere; even holding Becky's hand was difficult. I was in no condition for another fight.

"Up here," Becky shouted, and she led me down a long hall, narrow enough that we had to run single file. Becky was in front, and I ran behind her, glancing over my shoulder at the fast-approaching Ms. Vaughn.

Becky slowed to a stop, turning back to me with a quick confused look. The door was there, but it was just a regular wooden door, like all the others. She tried it. It was locked.

Ms. Vaughn was about forty yards away.

Becky shouted off the count. "One, two, three—"

Together we crashed into the door, and reeled back. It had hardly budged.

A second Ms. Vaughn appeared behind the first. And then an Iceman.

Becky and I tried the door again, and I heard a splinter, but it held fast.

"You're not getting in there," the front Ms. Vaughn said,

raising her Taser and approaching cautiously.

There was a scream down the hall—loud and angry. Both Ms. Vaughns turned just in time to see Curtis slam a rusty pick into Iceman's back. The android collapsed forward, instantly dead.

Carrie and Shelly appeared behind Curtis.

"Go!" Shelly yelled. "We'll take care of these."

Becky was grinning as our eyes met. We counted down again and then slammed our shoulders into the door, shattering the wood frame around the knob and falling into the room. I tried to jump to my feet and stumbled, colliding with a tall computer bank.

Becky was faster than me, throwing her back against the cracked door and shoving it closed.

The room was exactly how Birdman had drawn it. Tall computers—sleeker and stranger than any I'd ever seen—lined the walls. There was an audible hum, low and deep, and it seemed to come from everywhere, all at once.

Two men sat at the end of the room in swivel chairs that faced a thousand square screens. In the center of the screens—just as Birdman drew—was the large curved window. It bowed into the room, between and in the middle of the action. There was only darkness on the other side.

Neither of the men turned around.

"Bense," Becky said, drawing my attention back to the door.

There was a loud splintering crack as an android tried to come in after us. I leapt against the broken door, but it was a losing battle. Ms. Vaughn was too strong.

"Wait," Becky said, jumping to the side, to the computer banks. She put her weight against the first one—six feet tall and narrow like a filing cabinet. Just as Ms. Vaughn hit again, the computer tipped, sliding diagonally across the door.

"She'll just knock it over," I said, but Becky had turned to the two men.

"Call her off," Becky shouted to them. "Or that thing falls."

They continued to stare at their computers, seemingly oblivious to us.

Becky stepped back to me.

I waited for Ms. Vaughn, for the door to shake and the computer to fall. But it didn't come.

One of the men turned around. It wasn't Iceman. He was old.

"Well?" he said.

I stammered, looking down at Becky. She took my hand.

"Let them go," I said. "All of them."

"Or what?"

I knew his voice. It was the man who'd interrogated me, the man who'd laughed as Becky was being tortured.

I looked at her hand for the first time. There was a jagged

scar between two knuckles, now mostly healed and pink.

The man laughed. "You thought we were hurting a duplicate, but you were wrong."

"Who are you?"

"The truth," he said, "is that your little tirade about not believing it was her is what gave us the idea to send the duplicate in today. It didn't work, obviously, but you must admit it was a good idea."

Becky stepped to a computer, scowling at the man. "What button should I push first?"

"That depends on who you want to kill," he said, supremely confident.

He still hadn't stood up. He knew we were unarmed and weak.

"Don't forget that every one of your friends has an intensely delicate piece of technology in their brains. Smashing things—knocking over that computer, for example—could make you a mass murderer."

"I'd hate to take that title away from you," I said.

His mouth wasn't quite matching up with his words. It was like he was a bad animatronic. Maybe one of the first androids?

"Who are you?" I asked again.

"Who do you think I am?" he said loudly. "I'm God! I make life. I control it."

Becky shook her head and walked toward him. I followed.

"You destroy more than you create," I said.

"We've just been practicing," the old man said. "Getting better all the time. But things have finally started moving."

I looked at the screens as we approached, finally able to make out the small images. There were faces, landscapes—

"Each one of these is a dupe?" I said, pointing at the tiny monitors.

"Yes," he said. "We have quite a few. More than you thought?"

I stared. Becky's hand gripped mine a little tighter as we began to pick out things we knew—a glimpse of the front of the fort, a hallway in the school, Gabby's face talking directly toward a camera. But there were others—adults in houses, or cars, or on streets.

"Who are they?" Becky whispered.

I felt nauseated. This was bigger than I'd imagined.

I thought of the president's daughters. "Why are you replacing real people?"

"Does that surprise you?" he said. "We've been practicing since way back when we built that fort. We have a duplicate of every human in that town you were hiding in, and it never crossed your mind that we were trying to replace people? That was the whole point."

Up close, the old man didn't look real at all. His skin was obviously fake, like a Halloween mask.

"But why them?" I asked. "Why the president's daughters?"

The other android was still facing the front, but he wasn't doing anything. I wondered whether he could even move.

"What do you think?" the android said. "I want you two to really mull it over and try to think of a reason someone would want to control the president. Go ahead. I'll wait."

I peered into the black curved window. There was something on the other side. Just a shape out of the corner of my eye.

Becky reached out to touch the old man. He swatted at her hand, but he was awkward and jolting. He missed.

"Who controls you?" she asked.

I turned, looking for something. Something hard.

"What makes you think I'm not like the others? Like Ms. Vaughn?"

"You're too believable."

He laughed. "This is believable?"

"I mean your personality," she said. She wasn't afraid of him at all now, standing in front of the machine, touching his rubbery face and hands. "Ms. Vaughn and Iceman don't have humans attached to them. That's obvious."

"And you think I do?" he said. He was ancient. Whatever artificial skin he once had was now a mess. These androids hadn't been updated in decades. Maybe even a century.

"Nope," I answered, and I pushed the second, motionless

robot off his chair. He slumped to the floor without a twitch.

Becky looked confused, and the old man turned to me.

"Violence won't solve anything," he said, and laughed and gestured mechanically to Becky. "I heard her say that once."

"Who are you?" I asked. "Are you the first?"

"Do I look like anything other than a puppet?" he said. He gestured at the other android on the floor. "We're relics, from a time when this room was more necessary. Now it's all controlled remotely. A neural link straight to Mr. Maxfield." He laughed, as though he'd made a joke.

I picked up the chair the second man had been sitting in. It was heavy and unwieldy, but heavy was exactly what I wanted.

Becky touched my arm. "What are you doing?"

I nodded toward the curved window. "I can't smash the computers, so I'm going to smash that."

The old man swung at me, and Becky pushed him over onto his face. He flailed, trying to get up, and Becky jumped away from him. Ms. Vaughn banged on the door again.

"Count of three," I announced, knowing someone was listening. "One, two, three."

I crashed the chair into the glass, and it bounced off with barely a scuff mark. I slammed it again, with the same result.

"Bravo," the old man said, finally rolling onto his back.

"Hey, Bense." I felt Becky's hand on my arm, and turned to her.

She held out the two dropped Tasers, the box cutter, and the broken powerhead. They'd all been gathered on a shelf.

The old man laughed. "What did I say about damaging the computers? I don't think a Taser would be wise. And what will a box cutter do to a puppet?"

I set down the chair and picked up the powerhead. It was just the pipe and the bullet, the screwdriver having broken off in the hall.

I held the pipe to the glass.

"Hey, Becky," I said. "Find me something pointy."

The old man flailed at me again, but he was ancient and weak. He couldn't even stand.

"Would a pen work?" Becky asked.

"I don't know."

"Oh," she said. "Here. It came off when we moved the computer." She handed me a three-inch-long screw.

I positioned the screw at the back of the powerhead. I tried not to let my nerves show, but I was afraid I was going to blow my hand off.

And then it appeared.

There was a face in the window, obscured in the dark liquid. The two eyes stared back at us, and a slit of a mouth, but that was the only thing recognizable about it. The skin was red and patchy—almost like a leopard but more subtle—and it was smooth and sleek like a fish.

"What is it?" Becky whispered.

Something appeared—a tentacle, or a hand. It pressed against the glass for a moment, and then flashed away into the darkness.

"What the hell are you?" I stammered, nervously and quickly bending down to grab the screw.

The voice came from the old man, as the face faded back into the darkness. "Perhaps your astronomer Carl Sagan said it best. 'Somewhere, something incredible is waiting to be known.' You should consider yourselves lucky. This is a landmark moment in human discovery."

The old man, his rubbery skin, tried to smile.

I placed the powerhead against the glass again, and repositioned the screw.

"I don't care what you are," I said. "But unless you release every single human under your control, and shut down all the androids, I'll smash that glass and spill you all over the floor."

The face appeared again, the words coming from the old man. "I've worked too long for you to destroy it now."

"Tell that to the bullet," I said.

"Look," Becky said, pointing at one of the monitors. It was a security camera watching one of the underground halls. At least ten kids from the town ran past, all armed. Shelly and the others were taking over the complex.

The face disappeared, swirling out of sight. It was darting around inside the tank, agitated.

"Yes," he snapped. "All that interrogation, and I should have simply waited. The missing students tunneled down a few hours ago. They've been causing me no end of problems. I can kill them all right now if you'd like."

I tapped the powerhead on the glass, and the face flashed angrily again in the darkness.

"You think you've won, but you're fools," he screeched.

It reappeared, closer to the glass this time. I could see tiny teeth in its inhuman mouth, the rippling scales of its skin. It was grotesque.

"Do it," Becky demanded. "Now."

One by one the screens around us dimmed to black, and a moment later they turned back on, showing different images—live feeds from the security cameras. The students in the school were panicking, half their classmates seeming to drop dead beside them.

"The implants are disabled?" Becky asked, her voice quiet now.

"Yes," the old man snapped, his voice bitter and snarling.

"And the security? The gates and all the locks?"

"You're free to go!" he bellowed. "But know what you've done. The president thinks he has just witnessed both his daughters collapse and die, and when they try to resuscitate them—when they take them to the hospital and scan them and autopsy the bodies—they'll know the truth."

Becky seemed to tremble at the thought. "You did it," she said.

"We didn't start a war," he answered. "We were merely observing. You've incited a worldwide panic."

"We?" I didn't like the sound of that.

He laughed, one final defeated time. "I've heard you all theorize about it, and some of your guesses are less moronic than others. Maxfield Academy isn't the only training facility. Trying to replicate human behavior is different for teenagers than it is for adults, different for Americans than it is for Chinese."

"Let *everyone* go," Becky said.

"Oh, I don't have that kind of power," he said. "I'm only one of many."

The powerhead pipe was getting heavy in my weak hands. "I assume you have some way to escape?"

"I'm not staying here with you."

"Good," I said. "Because I'm smashing this glass in ten seconds. Becky, count it off."

She grinned and began the countdown. The face spun angrily in the darkness, a froth of black bubbles battering the glass. As she counted, Becky jogged back to the door and pushed the computer bank—now completely silent and dark—out of the way and watched it crash on the floor.

The liquid began to froth, and the level dropped steadily.

By the time she reached ten, there was only a foot of the black water left.

"Aren't you going to smash it?" she asked.

I looked back at her. "What if it's poisonous?"

"What if he comes back?"

I nodded, took a breath, and then punched the screw into the powerhead.

There was an explosion and I dropped the pipe. The glass didn't shatter completely, but a two-inch hole punched through, and cracks splintered across the tank.

Becky took my shaking hand. We watched the monitors. Students were panicking, but I saw one boy down on the main floor try a door. It opened. He called to the others.

"Come on," Becky said, pulling me toward the door. "They're going to need help. And we have to find Shelly and the others."

We stepped around the broken computer and pushed out through the splintered door. Ms. Vaughn lay lifeless in the hallway. Farther down was the Iceman Curtis had killed.

"I didn't think it would work," I said, letting go of her hand and pulling her next to me. The hall was narrow, but we didn't need to walk single file if we were really, really close together.

"I'm not sure what even happened," Becky answered.

The complex was silent and empty as we navigated the hallways back to the detention elevator. The alarm was off, but it felt eerie. We didn't know exactly what happened here, but we knew enough.

Someone turned the corner. Gabby. Blood was streaming from a cut on her forehead, but she was smiling happily. "You guys okay?"

"It's over," Becky said.

Gabby gave a whoop and turned back down the other hall.

I stopped, taking a moment to breathe.

"Do you think he was right?" I asked Becky. "Worldwide panic?"

"If there isn't now, there will be when we tell everyone what happened here, when we tell them what he said."

He. It. Whatever it was.

Becky squeezed my hand, and stopped. "You came for me."

I smiled, looking down at her. "I told you I would."

She put her arms around my neck. "I hear you're quite a kisser."

"I knew that wasn't you," I said, feeling my face flush.

"Sure you did."

I touched her side, my thumb pressing into her armpit.

"Hey!" She flinched away and laughed.

"Just checking."

ACKNOWLEDGMENTS

This book was written during one of the hardest times of my life, and I owe a lot to many people. Most importantly, I owe everything this book is, and everything I am, to Erin, who has stood next to me through every trial, held my hand through every trauma, and hugged me as I've cried.

I also owe my sanity to those who went out of their way to encourage me through some of my darkest days: Annette Lyon, Josi Kilpack, Jeff Savage, Larry Correia, Luisa Perkins, Dan Wells, and especially Krista Jensen. You're all amazing people.

Joel Hiller was instrumental to the creation of this story, brainstorming over lunches, escaping a job we both hated.

And a million thanks to my alpha and beta readers: my writing group, Sarah Eden, Michele Holmes, Annette Lyon, Heather Moore, Jeff Savage, Lu Ann Staheli; Ally Condie; Krista Jensen; and Dan Wells.

And thanks to Erica Sussman, my unbelievably awesome (and extremely patient) editor. And huge thanks to all the Harper team—Tyler, Christina, Arianna, Patty, and dozens more—who helped form this pile of words into a great book.

And never-ending thanks to Sara Crowe, who made this all happen.